FLIGHT TO VICTORY

ALSO BY RICHARD HOUGH

Captain Bligh and Mr. Christian
Edwina: Countess Mountbatten of Burma
The Fleet That Had To Die
Mountbatten
Razor Eyes

FLIGHT TO VICTORY

by Richard Hough

LODESTAR BOOKS
E. P. Dutton New York

This book is a considerably revised version of *B Flight*
by Bruce Carter (a pseudonym for Richard Hough), published
in 1970 by Hamish Hamilton Children's Books Ltd, with the
ISBN 241 01834 X.

Library of Congress Cataloging in Publication Data

Hough, Richard Alexander, date
Flight to victory.

Rev. ed. of: B flight. 1970.
"Lodestar books."
Summary: Sixteen-year-old Will leaves his home, his
school, and his youth behind to become a pilot in
World War I.
1. World War, 1914–1918—Aerial operations, British—
Juvenile fiction. [1. World War, 1914–1918—Aerial
operations, British—Fiction. 2. Great Britain—History
—20th century—Fiction. 3. War—Fiction] I. Hough,
Richard Alexander, date. B flight. II. Title.
PZ7.H8142Fl 1985 [Fic] 84-28596
ISBN 0-525-67159-5

Published in the United States by E. P. Dutton, Inc.,
2 Park Avenue, New York, N.Y. 10016

Published simultaneously in Canada by
Fitzhenry & Whiteside Limited, Toronto

Editor: Virginia Buckley Designer: Isabel Warren-Lynch

Printed in the U.S.A. COBE First Edition
10 9 8 7 6 5 4 3 2 1

for Will Garland

A glossary of unfamiliar words relating to aircraft, weaponry, and World War I begins on page 167.

Three of them came down the road almost side by side. There was not a yard between them. Tom Filton was in front, and Will could do nothing about it. Tom was just too fast for him, and that was that. But Will was holding off Jim Shore, the fishmonger's oldest boy. I won't be beaten by the fish, that's certain, Will told himself. The school gates were just in sight, and so was Vicky, sitting on the wall, neat and trim as ever.

This was an every morning game of dare that sometimes became serious. If you arrived one minute after the bell rang, you got beaten if you were a boy, and given one hundred lines to write if you were a girl. Girls were never late, least of all Vicky, who so much enjoyed for many different reasons watching everyone else arrive. Especially the boys who were on the dare, racing that last minute as narrowly as they could. There were six regular contestants, all big boys of sixteen, who often loudly claimed to the girls that they were going to add a year to their age and join the army. When seventeen-year-olds were machine gunners, airplane pilots, heroes with medals fighting in France, it was hard to be sixteen and still at school—and what was worse, a school with girls.

Will had been beaten by the headmaster the previous week. It was a disagreeable experience, and he did not want it repeated. Tom Filton was drawing farther ahead, and the last peal of the bell echoed back from the eastern slopes of the deep valley. They were all cutting it very fine. Cutting it fine! That's good, thought Will. Who cuts finest, the butcher's boy with his mutton, the baker's boy with his loaf, or the fishmonger's boy with his smoked salmon? A tradesman's trio, all looking for a spot of excitement and showing off to the girls. In a way, it was more dangerous and more heroic to lose the running race, because that meant you were more likely to go over the minute allowance. It all added spice to the morning event, for Vicky and everyone else.

At sixteen, you were as old as the twentieth century. At sixteen, you were the only son of the village baker at Amplethwaite in Westmorland, England. At sixteen, you were still—yes, still—at school, and a school with girls, a small private school where your parents paid fees because that was supposed to be more respectable. Only laborers' children went to the state school. At sixteen, you were aching to go, to do something with a better purpose than beating the one-minute limit at the Amplethwaite Private. And yet for Will, at sixteen, his mind flinched away from serious thought about a decision—a decision to join his father in the bakery or to be apprenticed to another trade. But above all, the alternative was the fearsome expectation of joining the colors and fighting in France, where Frenchmen, Britons, Canadians, Australians, New Zealanders, and Indians from

India were fighting to keep out the invading Germans. It was the constant topic among the village boys and had been since August 4, 1914, over two years ago now.

The slate roof of the school had become a blur, and Will's lungs felt as if they must burst through his ribs. He scarcely noticed that for the first time in his life he had passed Tom Filton. He certainly had no idea that he was a dozen yards ahead of the school's fastest runner. He saw, in quick succession, Vicky standing up on the dry stone wall, waving her orange tam-o'-shanter; Mrs. Venner emerging from the big double doors with the roster board in her hand; and the two lines, boys to the right and girls to the left, rapidly forming up.

Will hurled himself into position at the back of the line. He leaned forward momentarily, his hands on his knees, panting so hard that he thought he would be sick. But today he was a triumphant fifty-nine-seconder. Mrs. Venner was already counting heads and ticking off names. "Is that a boy at the back?" she was demanding in her chill voice. Will lifted his head, replied haltingly, "Yes, Mrs. Venner. Will . . . Thompson," and saw out of the corner of his eye that the other two were still in the road, where you had to remain once the roster had begun. So Tom Filton and Jim Shore were both due for a beating. Will was sorry about that because he liked both boys.

For the older children, recess was more of an occasion for conversation than for noisy games. They gathered in groups, usually the boys in their knickerbocker suits and lace-up boots on one side of the stony yard and worn lawn at the back of the school, and the girls in their white blouses and long serge skirts, breathlessly gossiping and knitting on the other side. The boys were full of talk about the Amplethwaite Games, the vicar's new Indian motor bicycle (he was a one, the vicar), and of course the war. The talk always came back to the war, especially on that cool, early autumn day of 1916 with its dark news of death five hundred miles away.

Will was one of the last to hear the bad news. The bell for the end of recess was almost due to go off when the pharmacist's boy, young Austin who was only fifteen, told him. "Rutter was killed last week, in his scout plane, so they say," he announced with an effort to make his voice sound more solemn than sensational. "Did you know?"

Will shook his head. "Poor old Rut." They did not last long once they got over there. Every week the *Gazette* carried a list of names of the local dead, wounded, and missing in France or one of the other fronts, or at sea. Sometimes they were people Will and his family knew. Sometimes they were very young. But not often were they as young as Rutter, whose father had a little business over near Ambleside. Rutter had been head boy last year. "I think I can say without fear of contradiction that Tony Rutter has been the most popular head boy in the history of our school," old Venner had said in his speech at the end of the summer term. "We all wish him well." Six months later, he was training to be a pilot in the R.F.C. And nine months after that, he was dead.

"Good chap, Rutter," someone behind Will was saying. "I'm going to kill ten Huns with my bayonet just for that. I'm going to put my age up when I leave. . . ."

Tom Filton and Jim Shore sauntered out into the yard after their beating and just as the bell was ringing. They were pale but cocky. "Nothing to it," said Jim, even before anyone asked him.

"You ran all right," said Tom generously to Will. "You

ought to have a go at the Junior Guide race at the games." The great event of the year, the annual Amplethwaite Games? Will laughed and shook his head. The cool dimness of the schoolroom closed about them all, the girls and the boys, the bright and the dull, the twelve-year-olds and the sixteen-year-olds, the fast runners who dared all, the boys who did not, and the girls who watched and chattered.

Will heard Mrs. Venner teaching geography to the girls in the next room. Her voice was louder than that of the puny little assistant master, whose lungs were not good enough for fighting in France and who strove to teach them some elementary solid geometry. Will listened even less than usual. This morning he was feeling rather odd, as if something demanding was going to happen and he must prepare himself for it. It made him uneasy. Life was difficult enough without changes, let alone demands. With one half of his mind, he wanted things to go on as they were; with the other half, he knew that they could not, and this meant that he had to face challenges.

Will looked out of the tall narrow windows. But things are always changing, he was thinking. Look at that sky. It had been clear and pale blue when he left home that morning, and at recess. Now there were dark clouds building up over the fells. And there had been another change already that day. Rutter was dead. He had come in second in the Junior Guide race at last year's games, and now he was buried near his smashed airplane somewhere in France.

And a third change. For Will had beaten Tom Filton down the road. He did not know how he had done it; nor, he suddenly realized with a flush of shame, should he be thinking of something so trivial in contrast with poor Rutter's death. He had been a real runner. He had not flinched from making decisions—brave decisions. . . .

And yet the rest of the school seemed to think that Will's run that morning was quite as important as the news of Rutter's death. During the day, several of the junior boys came up to him as if he had won a V.C. "You didn't give Tom Filton much of a chance," said one twelve-year-old breathlessly, and then ran away. Even Mr. Venner had heard about it, although his reaction was severe rather than congratulatory. "Understand you cut it rather fine this morning, Thompson. You know how strongly I feel about my pupils being punctual."

But the most important event occurred after school. Will with his bulging satchel across his back was walking down the gravel path to the gates with two other boys. Tom Filton was just ahead of them. Every now and again, he turned his red head to throw out some lighthearted remark, for Tom liked to keep the talk and laughter going. The girls were already in their groups by the gates, chattering away like sparrows, the knitters knitting away as if the soldiers in France at the fighting front would die of frostbite if the socks were not finished that night.

The ritual of leaving school was as clearly defined as the arrival. Most of the girls would chatter harder than ever as the boys passed, the boys kicking their boots in the gravel, swinging their satchels at one another, and barging shoulder against shoulder. Some of the girls watched them out of the corners of their eyes. Then a few of the older ones would answer back sharply at the boys, detach themselves from their group, and walk up the village street with a chosen companion.

It had been like this since Will could remember. When he had been only fourteen, he had once walked a little red-haired girl with braids back to her house and had been loudly jeered by his friends. For months he had blushed when he remembered the event. The girl had left Amplethwaite soon after, and now he could not even remember her name. He had never walked anyone home since. Tom Filton had a girl, of course, a pretty, fair-haired girl, Elizabeth. He treated her with grave respect, as if they had been married for years, and sometimes he went in and had tea with her parents. Tom picked her up from her group, took her satchel, and then they walked off together, his head bent down in deep conversation.

By chance, Will was alone when he went out through the gates. Vicky was sitting on the wall, dangling her legs and her tam-o'-shanter in exactly the same attitude as she had been in the morning when she had cheered his panting arrival and they had both joined the end of their roster line, just in time. Vicky had long, light, wavy chestnut-colored hair that fell below her shoulders, and a face that turned to a lovely matching color at the first touch of spring sunshine. Will knew that face as if it were his own. In his mind it was perfection. Those brown eyes that suddenly shone with excitement when the boys on the dare raced past in the morning! Sometimes when they chanced to glance in his direction, Will thought about nothing else for the rest of the day.

Vicky called down to him as he passed. "You ought to do the Guide race, Will Thompson," she said. He looked up at her. There were black clouds hanging over Langfell behind her head, but the last of the day was clearing the sky to the west, and the sun was breaking through all over Westmorland and shining on the left side of Vicky's face.

She was not teasing him. Her expression was serious. "You ought, really you ought," she said while he was still thinking how to reply.

"Oh, I'm not fast enough for that. Not nearly fast

enough." He remembered the word they used when they talked about the Guide race. *Stamina.* "I don't have the stamina, you see."

"How do you know till you try?"

Will remembered his manners and said formally, "It's very kind of you to be encouraging."

Then Vicky said something surprising, and he remembered her words for a long time. "I like first things," she said. "I like winners. It's time this school won the Junior Guide. Tony Rutter was second last year, but that's not first. Did you know that no one at school has yet won the Junior Guide? You could win it, though."

A girl on the other side of the wall was calling, "Come *on,* Vicky," as though she had said it several times already, and Vicky swung her legs over the wall and dropped down the other side without waiting for Will to answer.

At tea at Will's house, there was talk about the village fête last week, about the Amplethwaite Games in three weeks, and inevitably about the war.

Will's father grumbled about the quality of the flour he was getting, and there was a shortage of yeast. Because so many British ships were being sunk by German submarines, food was rationed, and that included bread. "It's no fun being a baker when there's a war on," said Will's father. He was a heavily built man with thick fingers, and his hands and arms were muscular from so many years of kneading dough. He did not usually talk very much, except to grumble. But he was reliable and steady and never became bad-tempered, like Tom Filton's father, who had a raging temper. Another good thing about Mr. Thompson was his devotion to Will's mother. He worshiped his wife and always smiled a great broad smile when she gently rebuked him for his grumbling.

"A war's no fun for anyone, dear," said Mrs. Thompson. Will had inherited his liveliness and restlessness, as well as his thin, taut body, from her. Will loved and admired his mother. He watched her dart over to the range and deftly refill the black teapot from the kettle. "No one enjoys a war," she added. "And don't forget how lucky we are here. It's the people in the towns who are going hungry. The factory workers and all. We're lucky, you not being allowed to join up because there has to be a village baker, and Will too young, thank goodness."

Mr. Thompson stirred his tea slowly and smiled up at her as she poured some more for Will. "Yes, we ought to count our blessings," he agreed. "And the war'll be over before they can call up Will."

"You're only a school lad, aren't you, love." She put in two teaspoonfuls of rationed sugar and handed him the cup with a smile.

Will did not mind being reminded by his mother that he was still at school because she did not make it sound patronizing. But the words *school lad* were still running around his mind while he was bringing in the two cows, which they kept in the two-acre field behind the house, for milking. He was a school lad, and Vicky was a schoolgirl. She had spoken to him today. She had told him she liked winners. And she had told him he ought to enter the Junior Guide race. Those were the facts of the day to be chewed over, for as long and as lovingly as Daisy and Cherub chewed their cuds.

Wednesday had been an eventful day, and so was Thursday. Thursday was also a day of decision for Will. It was a day that left him astonished at the speed with which things could happen, especially to someone who was used to hanging back when changes were in the air. Will got to school in good time, and while he talked to a friend outside the doors, he glanced several times in the direction of Vicky, who was at her place by the gates. But there was no racing that morning. Once during the school day, he caught a glimpse of Vicky. She was in the corridor, walking briskly along with a friend, her chestnut hair swinging. Her friend's voice sounded commonplace against the bell-like beauty of Vicky's. Perhaps it was this that made him decide that, if the chance came, he would ask if he could walk her home.

The enormity of this decision drove all thoughts of work out of his head for the rest of the day, and he wrote just two lines of a long essay in one hour. Even then, he was almost frustrated. Tom Filton, who was the cricket captain, decided that they must put in some practice that evening before their match against Grasmere on Saturday. But when the end-of-school bell rang, it was pouring rain. "We'll have to make it tomorrow night," said Tom when they were all packed on the porch, struggling with their raincoats.

Will was overcome with a mixed sense of dread and elation. Which did he hate more, the feeling of utter failure that would be with him for the rest of the day if he failed, or the agony of embarrassment of asking Vicky?

The rain relieved Will of the worst of the task. It was coming down so fast that it had become a merciful screen by the time he had put on his raincoat. Singly or in little screaming groups, the children ran out from the shelter of the porch into the downpour. Among them and, for once, alone ran Vicky. Will broke through a group of juniors who had not yet found the courage to take the plunge, and ran after her. She was running so fast that he lost her for a moment. He caught up with her near the post office, and he saw for the first time that she was not wearing a raincoat. Instinct seized Will, for he could never have planned what he did now. He came alongside her, grabbed her hand, and pulled her into the post office doorway.

She looked up at him in surprise and began laughing. The water was pouring down her face, her long hair was clinging to her cheeks, and her cotton dress was stained dark over her shoulders.

"That wasn't fair," she said and began laughing again. "I could have beaten you easily if I'd known you were behind."

"Why aren't you wearing your raincoat?" Will asked.

"Because I've lost it, silly. And I don't mind getting wet." She pushed some hair out of her eyes and looked out into the blinding rain. Was she looking for her friends? Will would have been half-relieved if she had seen them and fled. But no one was in sight, and in any case you could hardly see across the road.

"I'll be late for tea, come on," Vicky said, and pulled at Will's hand as naturally as if they had been friends for years.

"You're going to put on my coat," said Will firmly. He pulled his arms from the sleeves and held it out for her.

She looked at him uncertainly. Then she laughed. "Very gallant! You know I'm going to make it wet inside as well as outside, and we'll both go home soaked instead of only one of us." She sounded as if she was going to leave at once. Instead, she leaned back against the slate walls of the doorway and looked at Will.

"You know I couldn't really have beaten you just now. Nobody in the school could beat you. You're the best runner of them all."

"Thanks," said Will. "I'm not really . . ." He did not bother to finish. He knew what she was going to say.

"You've got to go for the Junior Guide. Go on. It'll please your Mum, and fancy the Amplethwaite Private winning! That'll stop the state school kids from sneering at us, saying we're too soft and rich to run." She put her hand against his and held it. She held it tightly, and it was cold and wet and magically soft. She put her face close to his as if to impel him to a decision. "Come on. You'll get a prize, you know. Nice silver cup, it is. I've seen it."

Too much was being said at once for Will to have time to think of a reply. "Well, I'll see . . ." he began.

"No, say yes now." The rain was still trickling from her forehead, into her brown eyes, and down her deep brown cheeks. It was true that she did not care how wet she was, and for once she did not look as if she was about to laugh.

"Oh, all right. But I'm not really good enough." And it's true, he was thinking as he spoke. I'll just be making an ass of myself.

"You are good enough, you are, you are." She was obviously pleased at her triumph and was laughing again. What a lovely pure laugh it was! "You're going to be a winner. I like winners." And she clutched his wet hand with her own cold wet hand and pulled him out of the porch into the downpour. They ran splashing down the road.

"Faster, faster," Vicky was calling breathlessly. Her sodden hair was streaming out behind her. Will began to run seriously, and soon he was pulling her along behind him, and she no longer had any breath to laugh with. "Oh . . . oh!" she was gasping above the sound of the beating rain.

Vicky gave up at last on the long hill up to the church where the water was streaming down like a beck in full flood. "No, no," she pleaded. Will slowed up, and she almost fell into his arms. "Yes . . . you'll win . . . all right," she said as soon as she could. She was standing in the middle of the road with her hands on her knees, just as he had rested yesterday in the lineup after beating Tom Filton. Her hair was hanging over her face, and her voice was muffled.

After that they walked home, no longer talking much and no longer holding hands, as if the purpose of the afternoon had been fulfilled and they could give themselves up to the feel of the rain. Vicky had been right; they were both soaked to the skin by the time they arrived at her house.

It was a gray slate detached house on a side road, with stables for about a dozen horses and outbuildings alongside. A little farther on there was a walled-off yard, and Will could just make out the pyramids of coal like the peaks of a miniature black mountain range. For Vicky's father was in coal. He had six red wagons each with FRED C. MASON FOR BEST COAL painted on the side, and a prosperous business in this part of Westmorland.

Mrs. Mason opened the door, although Will knew that they had a maid. She stared in amazement at the two soaked figures and then burst into peals of laughter. It was a lovely laugh, just like Vicky's.

"Well, you two are a right sight. Shake yourselves before you come in." She was still laughing when they were in the hall. Then she called out, "Ethel, bring two towels at once." She turned to Will. "You've been playing the gallant one to my silly Vicky, haven't you." She looked at Vicky. "Why do you always lose your raincoat?" She turned back to Will. "You're the Thompson boy, aren't you? Your father bakes nice bread. We always have it. Vicky, you should have been doing the introductions."

After that, they dried their hair with the towels in front of the drawing-room fire, and Vicky was sent up for a hot bath and a change of clothes. After refusing an offer of tea,

Will left, taking with him, very reluctantly, a big black umbrella.

"She's a nice Mum," he told his own mother at tea. "It's a nice house, too."

"Oh, yes, they're quite well-off people. There's money in coal. . . ." She prattled on, but Will only heard it as an accompaniment to the song in his heart.

It was not until they were washing dishes together that he remembered the other thing that had happened, and the enormity of the decision struck him so suddenly that he nearly dropped a cup. When he had settled himself, he said as casually as he could, "I think I'm going in for the Junior Guide."

"Oh," she said, without looking up. There was a long silence, and she let the water run away and rinsed around the sink before she spoke. "That's a dangerous business, love. Your father might not like it, and I can't say I do. You must ask him."

A dangerous business? Will had never thought of that. But, yes, he supposed that there was some danger in it, and runners did get hurt sometimes running up and down these rocky fells, across the rushing becks. A boy had been killed in the Junior Guide three years ago, falling down a ravine. And broken legs and ankles were quite frequent.

Will was up on the fells on Saturday afternoon. Tom Filton had said, "You've got to practice every day you can." So he had missed the last cricket match of the season and gone out after midday dinner wearing running shoes, shorts, and a thick jersey over his vest. He also carried his father's big silver watch, which had a second hand. After his father had given his permission for Will to enter the Junior Guide, he had encouraged him with a number of tips, for he had been something of a fell runner himself as a young man.

"If you've got no one to race against, then race against the watch," he had said. "You borrow mine, set yourself a time for going around Black Crag, and then go on beating it. If you're faster every time, you'll not be doing so bad."

Next week, Will intended to join the other competitors in full practice on the real course, but for a start he wanted to be on his own. He knew every inch of the way up Black Crag because he had often helped old Dove get down the sheep. From the big curve in the beck at the bottom of the valley, it was about seven hundred feet to the rocky crag itself with the cairn on top, and it was about as steep and rough going as the real course.

He placed the watch carefully on a hummock of moss beside a stone, and looked up the fellside. There were sheep dotted about on the grass between the yellowing bracken, and a group of about a dozen more on a lush slope close to the ghyll, a stream that tumbled white down the steep slope to the beck beside him. There were two stone walls to climb, as there were on the real course, and there were sharp outcrops to avoid if you were not going to risk breaking your skull.

Will plotted his route and then looked about self-consciously to make sure there was no one about. It was unlikely enough in this lonely valley three miles from the village. No one ever came up here except on sheep business. The air was still and close, and there were heavy clouds huddled about the peaks of the higher mountains toward Scafell. The only sound was the steady rumble of the beck beating over the rocks behind him on its way down to Amplethwaite and the distant sea.

Will crouched down for the start and waited for the second hand to work its way around to the zero mark. Twenty minutes to three exactly. He pressed the weight of his body into the soft turf and raced off. It was easy going at first, up a gentle slope toward the first dry stone wall, avoiding the bracken that could tear at his bare legs and slow him down. He hoisted himself up onto the wall, paused crouching at the top, and jumped into the peaty moss. Now the gradient was steeper, and he had to cut through some bracken and reeds before reaching stony ground. He crossed the ghyll at a leap, scattering the sheep. For two hundred feet, the going was rough and steep, and Will resorted to the action the runners used for the worst part of a climb, pressing his hands hard against his knees to get more power behind each step. He was panting hard by the time he reached the second wall and almost succumbed to the temptation to pause and catch his breath.

This wall was higher, a nasty one to climb from below, and Will had to search for projecting rocks to take first his hands and then his feet. From the top, he half fell into deep heather, picked himself up, fell on a concealed rock, and grazed his knee. It was nothing. There would be many worse falls than this before the race.

Will thought he had done pretty well so far when he pulled himself hand over hand to the top of Black Crag itself and paused for a moment beside the cairn. He could see Black Crag tarn five hundred feet below and, spreading away into the misty distance, blue gray strips of two lakes, Coniston and Windermere. The top of Coniston Old Man was shrouded, and so were all the fells above two thousand feet. It was so quiet that he could hear the beck below and the sound of a threshing machine at work in the next valley. There were rooks circling aimlessly nearly a mile away above the bare slopes of Whelm Scar, and high above them another black shape. It was flying with unusual steadiness, Will thought, like a gliding eagle, and before he took the first step on the downward run back, he looked at it again. It was growing larger. It was not a bird after all; it was an airplane.

Will forgot all about the second hand of the watch going around its dial. This was a sight he could not miss. He had seen a plane flying only once before when he had gone to Whitehaven in the horse bus with his father, and that was a seaplane that had looked like a large kite holding up a pair of canoes. He studied the shape carefully. At school all the boys huddled around the picture magazines with photographs and diagrams of the British, French, and German planes flying over the western front, and knew their shapes as well as any antiaircraft gunner. It was a tractor, with the propeller in front of the engine, not a pusher scout, which had the engine and propeller in the rear. It was a biplane, no mistake about that, now that it was nearer.

Will shaded his eyes and concentrated all his attention on the machine, which had started to turn and might soon be lost to sight. For a moment, he was certain that it was a Bristol Scout. The shape of the fuselage, and the rotary engine, which he could now clearly hear, sounding rather like the vicar's motorbike, confirmed this identification. He looked at the tail again. The fin shape was not quite right, nor the shape of the wings. It was not a Bristol—it was the new Sopwith. This was exciting news all right. Would anyone believe him? But Will was certain now that it was one of the latest warplanes, the single-seat scout, which had only just gone into service.

Suddenly the plane went into a steep bank, revealing its underside, and then into a dive. The sound of the engine rose higher as it gained speed. The pilot was diving steeply, straight toward the side of Whelm Scar. Was he out of control and about to crash? Should Will run for help? He waited in horror for the sight of the plane smashing itself to pieces on the fell. But instead he saw little spouts of earth kicking up from the fellside directly in front of the scout, and almost at once he heard the rattle of gunfire.

It was the first time Will had heard a machine gun firing, but there was no mistaking it. The pilot was testing his Vickers gun and giving himself some target practice at a rock at the same time.

The pilot pulled his Pup out of its dive just in time, soaring up again with its engine laboring after the scream of the dive. Its wheels skimmed the bracken and rocks; it raced over the summit and almost at once dropped out of sight and sound down the far side. Will waited several minutes for it to reappear, but it seemed to have gone forever.

He was feeling the cold now. There was a light wind blowing, and he was losing the heat from the hard climb. So he ran on the spot for a few seconds to ease the muscles of his stiffening legs and then began his run down to the valley.

When he got back to the beck, his father's watch showed the time as a quarter past three. No record for that run! If he had wasted ten minutes watching the plane, a good run on the course should take twenty minutes. He would try for eighteen.

Will was halfway up Black Crag when he heard the plane's engine again. It was already very close. He stared in wonder as it flew low down the length of the valley toward him. It must be doing over a hundred miles an hour, Will calculated, and was still descending so that it would soon be below him. A second later, he was looking down at it, right into the cockpit. He could see the pilot turn his head. Then to Will's delight, the pilot spotted him, grinned, and waved a hand in greeting.

He was past in a flash, banking his machine around the south side of Black Crag. Will could still hear the sound of the engine from the other side of the fell. At first it gave a steady note, then rose in pitch as if the pilot was diving, fell again, and suddenly cut out. It was much louder when Will heard it again perhaps five seconds later, but no longer even. It was spluttering like a car that will not start properly. The pilot was in trouble; Will was certain of that. He imagined him looking around for a flat place to land. But there was nowhere on the other side of Black Crag.

For a second, Will was the pilot of the Pup scout. After the joy of soaring over the fells and down the valleys, he was suddenly fearful yet helpless, struggling with the controls and searching desperately for the best place to crash-land amid the rocks and ravines below, all the time falling like a mortally wounded hawk.

The silence continued, and with every second that passed, a crash became more certain. He must be down now —he can't still be gliding, Will told himself, and he felt sick at the thought of that brave, smiling young man lying with a broken neck among the wreckage of his airplane. If only he had seen the crash, at least he could have gone to fetch help. Instead, he began to bound up the fellside at a speed that would have brought him in first even in the Senior Guide. He leaped over the high wall as if it were a low fence and clawed his way up through the bracken to the steepest part of the slope. He could hardly stand at the top and had to catch his breath before he could begin his search.

But no search was needed, for there it was, five hundred feet below him in the bottom of the next valley close to the tarn, like a toy hurled to the nursery floor by a petulant child. Will had never liked broken things, nor breaking them, and his first reaction was to cry aloud, "What a waste! That lovely new plane!"

The wreckage was spread over a length of about a hundred yards, beginning at the edge of a green bog that the pilot had overshot. One wheel lay by itself; then there was a long line of broken spars, a complete wing with one red-white-and-blue roundel staring up at the sky like the eye of a dead animal, an unidentifiable mess of wood and canvas with half the propeller beside it, and at the end of a long dark groove cut in the soil, the circular engine. At least there had been no fire. But where was the pilot?

It took Will less than five minutes to get down to the wreckage. The still air was heavy with the mixed scent of hot oil and hot metal, like the inside of a car when the hood is raised. He called out once and began to search for the pilot among the rocks and dying bracken. He found him in the rocky ravine cut by a ghyll fifty yards from the remains of the cockpit from which he had been flung. Will had never seen a dead man, but this is how he had imagined one would look, more limp than any sleeping figure, and with the legs oddly twisted. There was a long tear in his flying jacket but no sign of any wound or blood.

The reasons for not approaching any closer were coming rapidly to Will's mind. If the man was dead, there was nothing he could do for him. He should run quickly to the village policeman's house and then to his father. There was nothing he could do here. Even the exciting anticipation of telling his friends was forgotten.

But he knew well enough where his duty lay, and he climbed reluctantly down the steep side of the ravine and stood above the still figure. The man's face was half-buried in the cold, clear running water. Will reached down and touched his shoulder. It was a disagreeable feeling, but he knew that he could not leave him like the sheep corpses he had often found in the ghylls at the end of a long winter. There were chips of broken glass from his goggles lying on the rock above the man's head; and for the first time that day, a shaft of brilliant sunlight broke through the clouds and sparkled on the glass and on the miniature waterfall feeding the pool. With an effort, Will pulled the man over and saw his face close up for the first time.

It was like the face of a boy, and he could not have been more than nineteen or twenty. Both eyes were shut, and one was circled by a massive black bruise. There was also a deep cut across his forehead below the line of his helmet, and the blood that had been staunched by the flow of cold water began to ooze heavily from the wound. There was also a shallow cut in the snub nose, and both lips were swollen and blue.

Will held the head in his arms for a moment, no longer afraid but filled with a sense of acute tenderness. A broken plane, and a broken life. He looked down at the man's legs and wondered if he could drag him from the ravine. When he looked back at the face, one blue eye was open and looking up at him.

"I just waved to you," the pilot said in a soft voice. His bruised lips shaped painfully into a caricature of the grin Will had seen from afar only a few minutes earlier. "You look as if you thought I was dead."

Will could only just hear the words. "Sorry to give you a shock, but I'm quite pleased, really." His lips and one blue eye closed as if the effort was no longer worthwhile.

"Which part of you hurts?" Will asked.

"Everything," the man whispered. "Legs, tum, arms, and head. Especially head. And I'm cold as hell." His eye opened again, but he did not try to smile. "Get something over me and go and fetch help. You look as though you can run, so run fast."

Will did not try to pull him farther out of the ravine where he was dry now, and looked around for something to cover him with. He could offer him nothing, as he was wearing only his running shorts and vest, but there was a lot of stiff, torn canvas from the fuselage of the Pup and one of its wings. So he tore off some lengths and wrapped them around the body of the pilot, who fell into unconsciousness again before Will ran off, past the wreckage and down the valley toward Amplethwaite.

Vicky was within earshot of the group of junior boys gathered around Will on Monday afternoon. He wished she would go away and join her own friends. He felt silly being treated as a hero when he had done nothing at all.

"Did he have a V.C.?" asked a freckled-face boy they all called Carrot.

"I don't know. I don't even know his name. He might have been a test pilot," Will answered, and tried to move away.

But the use of the term *test pilot* only further impressed the twelve-year-olds. For the present, he was their hero. Every boy in the village had been up the valley within an hour of Will's raising the alarm. Two of the fastest, now regarded as only slightly less heroic than Will, had got there before the policeman and had made off with armfuls of mementos—a fragment of the beautifully polished wood propeller, a strip of canvas off the broken wing, a segment of the roundels in the corner, and a complete strut with bits of bracing wire still attached. Others had spent the whole of Sunday searching Whelm Scar for machine-gun bullets and had come back with only a few newly chipped fragments of granite.

The incident that had brought the violence of the war closer to the village than ever before, and that had also brought joy to the boys who had followed every inch of progress of the Royal Flying Corps truck collecting the wreck and fame to Will, would be half-forgotten by the middle of the week and a remote memory by the time of the games. Will knew he should be savoring his brief moment of glory, but he was already tired of it. There was Vicky, obviously waiting to be walked home, smiling when their eyes met, pleased to see him the center of so much attention.

Will pushed through the junior boys and joined her, taking the satchel from her shoulder. "Bill Stokes wants you," Vicky said. "It's likely a telegram from the king, singing your praises." She laughed and led the way to the school gates where the odd-job boy from the post office, who bicycled about the village with telegrams when he was needed, was waiting for him. He opened his little black pouch when he saw Will and pulled out a buff envelope addressed to William Thompson, Esq. Will tore it open and read aloud to Vicky and Bill Stokes, who had already read it an hour before at the post office.

> LIEUTENANT SANDERSON THE PILOT YOU RESCUED MOST ANXIOUS YOU VISIT HIM AT NUMBER TWO NORTHERN DISTRICT GENERAL HOSPITAL PRESTON. (SIGNED) MEDICAL SUPERINTENDENT IN CHARGE

"You're the lucky one," said Vicky. She was pleased about it, Will knew. She was pleased because he was pleased.

"You'll have to give up an evening's practice to go to Preston," Vicky said.

Will realized that, and said so. "You can always do a bit extra the evening before and after," Vicky said encouragingly.

He left her at her gate and hurried home to change, trying to keep his mind clear about his training plans for that evening. But there were a lot of other things to think about, too many for comfort, in the past and in the future. And above them all—above the crashing of the plane, the stretcher party carrying away the pilot, the telegram in his pocket (the first he had ever had), the visit to Preston he must make, even the mixed dread and exhilaration he felt for the imminent Junior Guide—above them all stood Vicky herself, suddenly and magically *his* girl, expecting much from him.

Even Mr. Venner could not turn down Will's request to leave school after midday dinner. The telegram was, after all, a call to patriotic duty. So Will made the long bicycle journey to Windermere and took the afternoon train to Preston, carrying with him a parcel of home produce for Lieutenant Sanderson: a dozen dark brown speckled eggs, a pot of cream, and three carefully selected eating apples—all produce from their two acres.

It was still a long way to France from Preston, but in the city's streets you could feel the presence of the war closing about you. Signs pointed to the recruiting station, posters appealed for volunteers for war work, for economy of food and fuel, and there were patriotic slogans among the window displays in the shops. There were soldiers walking along the streets off-duty, and Will saw a marching column with rifles led by a tall, fierce corporal. Nearer the hospital, he met some men in hospital blue, the uniform worn by those who had been wounded. They were sufficiently recovered to go out in the autumn sun, some in wheelchairs or leaning heavily on the arm of a nurse, some with a leg missing and on crutches, all with faces of men who have known suffering and fear and were learning to cover the past with an expression of hope they might not yet feel.

The pilot was in one of a number of temporary huts built on the grounds of the old infirmary. Will was conducted down a long passage by the ward sister who seemed to indicate that if one of her patients was to be visited at all, it should be by no one below the rank of a field marshal. "He's very poorly still, and you mustn't stay more than half an hour, and talk quietly," she said briskly before opening the door to a mixed smell of disinfectant and floor polish.

Lieutenant Sanderson was lying with his bandaged head on two pillows, and one of his legs, covered in plaster and with a red woollen sock over the foot, was raised on a cradle. On a table beside the bed was a vase of russet chrysanthemums and a silver-framed photograph of a beautiful girl. His eye was blacker than ever and still half-closed, but the lips were less swollen, and he could smile a welcome. In spite of this, Will still felt uneasy looking at a face he had once believed belonged to a dead man.

The pilot raised a hand and pointed at the only chair beside his bed. "It is very kind of you to come all this way," he said. He had a south of England accent and drawled his words. "And there's not much to see now you've arrived. I think I must have been off my nut when I asked the doc. I was blathering away all sorts of rubbish after I came around, so the sister says. Funny thing, the head, when it goes wonky." He fixed Will with his one clear blue eye. "How did you skip school? Did they make a fuss?"

"That was all right, sir," said Will.

"Don't 'sir' me," said the pilot. "You look nearly as old as me. My name's Hugh. What's yours?"

Will told the pilot about the excitement the crash had caused, and made him laugh about two of the boys stealing bits of the plane before the policeman could get up the valley. He was especially interested to hear how they got the wreckage down from the fell and how they had covered the engine and machine gun with a tarpaulin because the Sopwith was still a secret plane.

"Secret my eye!" said Hugh. "Everyone knows about the Pup, though she's still pretty new. Do you know, it was my first time up in one, and I have to go and wreck the poor old girl. I've done nearly a hundred shows over the lines," he continued, referring to offensive flights against the enemy in France, "without the engine missing a beat, and then I go and lose my engine five hundred miles from the nearest Hun. Never touched by Archie or a Spandau bullet, and then I get whacked by a bit of Westmorland rock. That's life."

Will was uncertain whether it was the right thing to say. Was it bad manners to ask, or against regulations to answer? But he could not resist the temptation. "Have you shot down any Germans?"

"Six and a quarter so far." Hugh Sanderson laughed quietly. "Oh, it's all right, I didn't let the other three-quarters get away. Four of us had a go at a Fokker, and we all hit it before it went down. Just let me out of this stupid bed and I'll get that score up to double figures. It'll be easy with the Pup, make mincemeat of Fokkers with a Pup. There's a real scout for you, nippy in the turns and does everything before you have time to think—just like a good thoroughbred mare."

The pilot had run out of words. He lay still, his one good eye staring wearily at the ceiling. Will wanted to hear him talk again, and he wanted to ask him many questions. But he remembered the sister's words of warning. Hugh Sanderson's depleted energy was obviously spent, and Will knew that he ought to go. He stood up and held out the basket his mother had made up. "Here are a few things for you," he said.

The pilot turned his head slowly and smiled. "You're a kind kid," he said softly. "And I haven't even thanked you yet for saving my life. That's why I asked you to come. You pulled my battered old head out of the water—death by drowning in a stream. That'd be a nice finish."

"I only ran for help," said Will. "And that was good practice for the Junior Guide race next week."

"If you run as fast as you were going up that mountain when I flew past, you'll win all right."

The sister was at the door. "Time for you to leave, young man," she said severely.

"Ah, there's the old torturer again," Hugh Sanderson

said. "Always fussing and giving me hell and driving away my friends. Give the fellow a quid out of my wallet, will you, old torturer?"

Will backed away in embarrassment. "I don't want any money, really I don't. I liked coming."

"You obey orders or I'll have you court-martialed. Or I'll set the old torturer on you—that'll be worse. You're not paying your train fare to come and see an old beaten-up crock in hospital." He had regained his spirits and his strength. "That quid will do for two journeys, Will. Come and see me again. You look as if you'd make a wizard pilot, and I can give you some tips."

Hugh Sanderson's teasing had done the sister good, and outside in the corridor she became more friendly. "I've seen a few patients in my time," she told Will with a giggle, "but I've never known one make such a recovery. We thought he was going to die on Saturday night, and this morning he threw a pillow at me. Those flying lads are all the same—never stop their jokes."

The hospital sister's opinion of fliers was confirmed at Preston station, where Will waited for the train back to Windermere. There were a lot of soldiers in khaki and sailors in blue uniforms standing about on the platforms with their duffel bags, going back on duty after leave. Some of them were drinking cups of tea, and all of them were making a lot of noise. Suddenly from the far end of the platform there appeared the noisiest group of all. There were only four of them, all young R.F.C. pilots with wings sewn onto the left breast of their jackets, and they were making more noise than all the rest as they pushed a steel-wheeled luggage trolley along at high speed. Sitting on it was the stationmaster, in his smart blue uniform with brass buttons. His gold-braided hat was askew, and he was protesting in as dignified a manner as his ridiculous position allowed. The pilots were singing at the tops of their voices, "We *hate* the London North Western Rotten Railway!"

And as they went past, clattering and singing, Will heard one of the officers call out to the protesting stationmaster, "You'll get out when the train gets in, old boy!"

Will's train steamed in, and he saw no more of the boisterous party. "They never stop their jokes," the sister had said. In this case he could not help feeling sorry for the poor stationmaster, but her words seemed to be true. And what had been Hugh Sanderson's parting words? "You look as if you'd make a wizard pilot, and I can give you some tips."

Will did not once glance at his book all the way back to Windermere. He stared out of the window, and over and over again, like five scouts tirelessly looping-the-loop, the same series of subjects kept going around and around his mind: flying, war, Vicky, Junior Guide, sixteen-year-olds, flying, war, Vicky . . .

It was dark when he got home, and his mother had kept some supper hot for him in the oven. "How was the poor lad?" she greeted him.

"Not bad," said Will. "Much better. He thanked me for saving his life and said I'd make a wizard pilot and that he'd give me some tips."

His mother said nothing, and later that evening before he went to bed, he saw her sitting alone staring at the fire, saying nothing, doing nothing, which was not at all like her.

The Amplethwaite Junior Guide racecourse was one of the toughest in Westmorland. It was not as bad as the men's, which climbed to nearly twelve hundred feet and had broken the heart of many a tough shepherd and farmer, but it was just as steep and rocky. The guide races were the culmination of the Amplethwaite Games that were held on the third Saturday in October, and included wrestling, high jumping, sprinting, and the hounds' and puppy dogs' trails around the fells, on which the locals always staked more than they could afford. For every boy in the Lake District between fourteen and eighteen, the Junior Guide offered the chance to prove publicly his strength and bravery. Anyone who finished with the first ten was the subject of hero worship among his friends, and the girls, and walked with a new swagger for weeks after. The name of the winner was remembered for years.

Will had done well in the Junior running events last year, coming in fourth in the 220-yard sprint, and second in the

100. But there was little fame to be gained from the flat races, and very different qualities were needed for the seven-hundred-foot run up Amplethwaite Fell, around the flagpole on the rocky summit, and the sickening, stumbling descent back to the cheering crowds and the packed grandstands.

It was a cool, clear evening, four days before the event, when Will stood for the first time in his running gear with the other entrants at the starting line for a practice session. He felt calmer and more confident than he had expected. Just to have your entry accepted was a boost to any boy's spirits because the sports committee allowed only thirty boys to enter, and each candidate was considered on his record and from reports gathered informally from Amplethwaite and the surrounding villages.

There were two more factors that helped to lift Will's morale. First was the encouragement of his father, of Tom Filton, and of course, of Vicky. The second, which was less tangible and of which he was only half-conscious, was the confidence the wounded pilot, Hugh Sanderson, had shown in him. At the hospital last week, Will had only mentioned the Junior Guide to him. It was not the words "you'll win all right" that counted so much for Will as the whole experience of talking on equal terms with the pilot and of entering briefly his world of masculine gallantry.

After leaving Vicky and Tom and Elizabeth in the small crowd of spectators, Will joined the other boys gathered about the supervisor and his own father, who was acting as timekeeper. He found that he could talk easily with the boys he knew by sight from his own village, and even with one or two tough-looking strangers who had left school and had been working at a trade or on the farms for as long as three years. Will felt much of his shyness and uncertainty fall away now that he was a member of this select group.

"There aren't any rules about this practice," the supervisor was saying. "You can start off with someone else if you want to, and if you want to be timed, ask me or Mr. Thompson here. Any of you seen playing rough—barging or tripping or anything like that—will be ordered home and disqualified from the race. One piece of advice: Don't take risks or overdo your running. If you hurt yourself or strain a muscle, there's no time to get fit for Saturday."

The group broke up. Some of the boys went straight to the starting line and set off on an easy, warming-up climb. Will joined a dozen or so others on the smooth grass of the ring to limber up and stretch his muscles. The big lad from Ulverstone was already there. Tom had warned Will about him. He had come in third last year, and was now twelve months older, more experienced, and more muscular. "His name's Buxton, he works in the shipyard at Barrow, and he goes like the wind. But his weight's against him, and you can beat him all right." Will was not so sure. Buxton's calf muscles—and they counted for a lot—were immensely powerful, Will noted, as the boy (but he looked more like a grown man) ran past. There were others to watch, but Buxton had been tipped as the most likely winner.

"Take it easy, son," Will's father told him at the starting line. "Last year's winning time was twenty-two minutes. If you keep some strength in reserve and do it in twenty-three, you'll have some idea what you ought to be doing. Off you go—*now.*"

Will sprinted away alone from the line, into the field at the foot of the fell, and over the stone bridge. Above the trees ahead of him, he could see scattered white figures, some slowly and painfully making their way up, others traveling at startling speed already on their way down like frenzied ants heading for their nest. In the wood it was slippery underfoot from recent rain and the leaves. A fall cost you five seconds—that was what they said—allowing for the time it took to pick yourself up and regain your speed.

This part of the course followed the footpath, and the wall at the edge of the wood had large projecting stones set into it to form a stile. Before dropping down the other side, Will glanced back. By chance or plan, Buxton had set off shortly after him and was pounding up through the wood fifty yards behind. Should I rise to the challenge? thought Will, although he knew as he asked himself the question that there was only one answer.

There was steep, slippery turf across a field for the next few hundred feet. One of the first starters skidded as he went past Will on his way back, fell heavily, and rolled over and over before he could stop his momentum. He got to his feet as if nothing had happened; falls were harmless enough here. It was higher up, among the rock outcrops, where you could damage yourself.

Will became conscious of Buxton close behind him on one of the steepest sections, after he had climbed the second wall and about three hundred feet from the summit. To look back deliberately seemed to suggest an anxiety he should not show, but the big youth must be quite near because Will could hear the sound of his panting above his own breathing, and the steady *pad-pad-pad* of his footsteps. Will did a quick zigzag up a specially steep slope, and this allowed him to catch a glimpse of Buxton out of the corner of his eye. Yes, he was only just below and gaining fast on Will.

Will held him off until just below the summit and the flagpole; then Buxton went past in a thundering rush, and Will caught a glimpse of big, freckled, white-skinned shoulders and hairy calves that were thrusting his feet into the fellside like a pair of steam-powered rams in the Barrow docks.

It was on the downward run that Buxton, with his heavier weight, seemed to have the greater advantage. Once around the flagpole, the distance between them opened up. Buxton skidded on his way through a bracken path, stumbled, and fell heavily. He was quickly up again, covered in mud, but now Will was alongside him. Will saw the square-jawed tough cast him a glance of utter contempt before he leaped off into space from the top of a high outcrop, landed safely far below, and carried straight on through a patch of reeds and scattered boulders.

Will never caught up with him again. Back at the arena, Tom Filton ran up and put his coat around Will's shoulders and wiped his mud-soaked sweating face with a towel. The two girls, huddled against the evening chill, told him he had done well. Will smiled quickly at Vicky before asking his father his time.

"Twenty-three fifty. That's not so bad for first time out. Give yourself a ten-minute break before your second run." His father had just the right manner for the occasion, casual but obviously deeply interested in Will's progress and welfare. "Give him that lemon and water in the bottle," he told Tom before he returned to his duties at the line.

A lot of the boys were resting, each with a backer or two looking after him, and one or two having attention from Miss Neville, the village nurse, who was always present with her liniments and bandages.

Tom poured the sharp-tasting drink into a mug. "I've never seen so many bad runners as this year," he said encouragingly. "Some of that first lot could hardly *walk* to the top. Then they strolled down as if they were visiting Auntie on Sunday."

The girls laughed. Vicky was sitting on the bench close beside Will as if seeking the warmth of his overheated body.

"It's the war," said Will. "There are hardly any over seventeen this year. They're all off at the front."

But Will knew, as Tom knew, that there were still some very fast runners in the Junior in spite of the war. Buxton was not the only threat.

Will took off his overcoat and walked back to the starting line. Buxton was nowhere in sight. But Will had noted that neither his father nor his friends had mentioned the fact that Buxton had started off after Will and beaten him to the line by a good fifty yards. Of course he had been following his father's instructions not to go full out. Or had he, when Buxton was close behind on the last steep slope? Will preferred not to think about the matter. "Forget the others. Keep your mind on your legs" was his father's advice.

At the line his father said, "Knock off those fifty seconds this time." Will heard the click as he started the watch, and sprinted away again. He felt fine. He enjoyed the way his muscles worked in perfect unison, his lungs took the strain, and his feet gripped the damp ground. He went through the wood very fast, and at the top of the wall he saw he was gaining rapidly on three boys of about his own age and size who had started together before him. He quickly caught up with two of them and left them behind. The third held on for longer, but Will passed him, too, a hundred feet from the summit.

He swung around the flagpole and began the steep descent, leaping from rocks or grassy hummocks, his eyes picking out stage by stage the most favorable route. He made for the same outcrop from which Buxton had leaped, soared through the air, and landed safely. Farther down he found himself going too fast and nearly stumbled into a narrow ravine, but held himself just in time and hurtled on. When he reached the higher of the two walls, he knew he was making good time. Rushing through the wood, he thought he might even be making a record. He had nothing left in reserve when he reached the last flat stretch. Dimly ahead of him, he could see a group of figures clustered around the line. He charged toward them as if they were an enemy whom only the speed of his thrust could kill, and shot past them before collapsing in a heap on the turf.

Tom was helping him to his feet, and Vicky was soon beside him, holding his arm and wiping his face with the towel. "That was better, much better," Tom told him when he had got his breath back.

"Your father said twenty-two minutes forty-five seconds," said Vicky. "And he said well done. And so do I."

Will was confused by the mixed feelings that swam into his mind at this news. He was pleased that he had broken twenty-three minutes, and that it was possible to knock more than a minute off his earlier time when he had tried hard against Buxton. But the race had been won in just twenty-two minutes last year, and poor Tony Rutter had been only a few yards and a few seconds behind to take second place. Will doubted whether he could ever bring his time down by that margin.

Vicky did her utmost to dispel Will's doubts. At her suggestion, Will went around to her house that night. Her father and mother were there, and they all played bezique in front of the fire until ten o'clock. They treated him as if he were one of the family and laughed at his jokes and asked him about the pilot and told him that all the other entrants for the Junior Guide might just as well stay at home on Saturday and not bother to try the impossible feat of beating

Will Thompson. He even won twice at bezique and was feeling happy and cheerful when it was time to leave.

Vicky came to the door and out into the night with him. She was wearing a long pink dress, and her hair was tied back by a broad pink bow. Every time their eyes met during the evening, Will had felt a warm fire tearing through his body as if he had run ten miles in ten minutes.

"See you tomorrow evening at the arena," Will said. It was a pitch black night, and he could only just see her standing by the gate a few feet away, faintly silhouetted by the light from the curtained windows behind her.

Vicky did not answer for a moment, and Will said, "You will be there, won't you?"

He could see that she was standing quite still. "Yes," she said, and made no move to return to the house.

"You'll be cold, Vicky." What a lovely name it was! He remembered how she had taken the coat from Tom and put it around his shoulders after the second run. Now it was she who needed it, though her face and body still felt warm in the chill night air when he reached around her shoulders.

The heavy coat slipped and fell to the gravel path. He began to laugh but before he could pick it up they fell into each other's arms as if it was something you always did before picking up anything from the ground. They did not kiss. There did not seem to be any need to kiss. Their cheeks were pressed hard together, and this seemed to be the only possible communication between them, with her warm breath playing softly against his neck.

Will did not fully understand what had happened until he heard the crunch of her feet on the gravel and saw her briefly in the shaft of light from the open door.

The house was silent when he came back five minutes

later for his forgotten coat, which lay a crumpled dark shape on the ground, and the only lights came dimly from the upper windows.

"Hold on a sec," called out the voice from behind the door in answer to Will's knock.

Will heard a sharp cracking sound. Hugh Sanderson shouted, "Come on in, old boy. Don't hit that table. Things are a bit congested in here."

Will saw at once why there was scarcely room to squeeze along to the bed in the corner of the diminutive room. The pilot had somehow acquired a lightweight card table on which were vertically balanced two mattresses to provide a double thickness. Pinned to the top mattress was a large sheet of white board on which were depicted the rough silhouettes of a number of German airplanes. Surrounding each machine were numerous small puncture holes, originating from the object in Hugh Sanderson's hands. It was a black Webley air pistol. In front of the girl's portrait on the bedside table was a large box of slugs. "Got to keep my hand in somehow," he said. "You have a go."

Will had handled a 12-bore shotgun since he was about ten and was a fair shot against rabbits and squirrels, but he had never fired a pistol. He raised the loaded weapon and gazed along the sights.

"Try and get that Hun in the Aviatik—the gunner. He's been eluding me for hours, and I know he's going to get in a burst at me if I don't get him soon."

Will picked out the Aviatik from the Albatros C1, the Fokker monoplane single-seater, and the three other German machines on the board. The Aviatik had been shot down a dozen times, but there was not a single hole within an inch of the observer in the second seat.

The first shot went clean through the pilot. "That's a waste, I've done him in hours ago. The observer's flying the airplane now, as well as observing."

Will took long and steady aim and pulled the trigger. It was a bull's-eye—clean through the blurred outline of the figure. Hugh Sanderson beat his hands on the bedclothes. "Dead shot!" he exclaimed. "Why couldn't I do that?"

Will sat down and asked the pilot how he felt. "Bored stiff," he said. "I can't stand this dump much longer. My head's nothing, just a spot of concussion and a crack on the skull. It's this darned leg. It's a multiple fracture of the thigh, or that's what they say. But it feels all right, so I wrote to the C.O. today and asked him if he could get a Pup fixed up so that I can work both rudder bars with my left leg."

"Are you reequipped with Pups yet?" asked Will. He suddenly saw in his imagination a dozen of those beautiful little scouts taking off together and heading in a fury of engine noise for the German lines. "What are they like to fly?"

For an answer, Hugh Sanderson raised his right hand and held it outstretched flat above the sheet. He suddenly twisted his wrist one way then the other. "Quick as that on the controls. We'll make mincemeat of the Fokkers with them. All we want is fifty more horsepower and another Vickers. Sometimes it's tough having only one gun against the Hun's two."

They settled down for a long, concentrated airplane chat. Hugh Sanderson's squadron had been flying D.H.2s, a single-seater "pusher" scout armed with a single fixed Lewis gun. Will could almost draw its shape in detail by heart. All the boys at school knew about the D.H.2, and during recess the juniors would pretend they were sitting in the forward mounted cockpit nacelle, one hand on the joystick, the other on the single Lewis gun, making suitable noises. The D.H.2 was a nice little bus, the pilot said, a bit skittish like a good colt, but tameable—if you did not spin and crash first. "We needed them all right. Before the D.H. came along, the Fokkers were cutting the air to pieces. Now we've got wind that the Huns are going one better, but we're going better than them with the Pup." He toyed with the air pistol as if it were the deadly Vickers machine gun he had fired harmlessly at Whelm Scar only a week before.

What did it feel like to swoop down on a German scout, to take aim, and watch the bullets striking home? What did you do to loop-the-loop or get out of a spin? How did you get out of the way of a German when he had you in his sights? Will's mind was full of questions about the mysterious, exciting world above the skies of the western front. But only a few of the answers satisfied him. Hugh Sanderson's conversation was full of flying jargon, full of tales of practical jokes in the mess when dud weather kept them on the ground, and of lighthearted references to Bill and Jack and Charlie, who had racked up big scores, come back wounded with their airplanes like colanders, or gone down in flames behind the lines.

It was all fascinating to hear, but only twice did the pilot say something that brought to Will's mind a clear picture of an event in which he felt he was participating. "The clouds were spinning like a blessed top," Hugh Sanderson said at one point. "The only way I could think of getting away from them was by going into a spin. I tried to get out of it before I went into the clouds, but the old machine wasn't having any, and on the other side of the clouds it was the ground that was spinning, and it wasn't far away either. Well, I kept the stick forward and held opposite rudder till I thought my leg would break—and out I came in a steep dive. And what do you think there was just under my nose? A blooming Aviatik, just like that"—and he pointed at the cardboard target at the other end of the room—"plodding along like a Hammersmith bus on a Sunday morning. If I'd shut my eyes, I couldn't have missed."

Then Hugh Sanderson said something that Will thought about for a long time afterward. "Poor devils, they didn't even have time to mutter a prayer."

Will looked at the face of the young pilot who had killed men at close range and had himself missed by inches many enemy bullets, who had seen the occupant of that Aviatik collapse forward on the gun he had had no time to fire, and who had watched the others struggling helplessly to get out of a burning cockpit before dropping like a streaking funeral pyre into the trenches below.

Will did not know how to frame his next question, but he longed to know the answer. At last he got out the words clumsily. "What do you think about the Germans—I mean, all of you on the squadron—what do you think?"

"We don't, we just shoot 'em before they shoot us," Hugh Sanderson answered lightly and laughed. "If you start thinking, they've got you." He took aim with the pistol and put a slug dead center into the Fokker pilot. "Not bad. No, the Hun's all right. Same sort of chaps as we are. We had a prisoner in the mess one night about a month ago. He got a couple of fouled-up plugs in his engine and couldn't get away when our C.O. found him about a mile off. He went in at the edge of our field. Wasn't hurt at all. When we got him really drunk, we all sang the German national anthem, and then he stood on the table and chanted "God Save the King"—every darned verse. Can't think where he learned it. I wouldn't have minded flying with him, but of course that wouldn't have done." The pilot laughed again.

"Wouldn't have done at all. Somebody's decreed we're enemies, and that's that.

"Enough of all this rubbish." He turned a sympathetic eye on Will. "How's the practice going? You're going to lick 'em tomorrow, aren't you?"

Will was pleased that the pilot had remembered the day of the games. "I don't know about that, but I'll have a go."

"Yes, have a go. But make sure you go first. I don't want you coming back next week and telling me you were a good second. Winning—that's what counts in this life." He turned toward the opening door and groaned. "Look out, here she comes. What unspeakable tortures have you got for me this morning?" he asked the sister, who carried a hot drink on a tray.

"The doctor's coming to examine your head in a minute," she said.

"It's his head that needs examining," Hugh Sanderson answered smartly. "Nothing wrong with mine except this bandage is too tight. It puts me off my jolly old aim."

Will's father said, "The last five minutes before the start is the worst part, lad. Make your mind a blank and just keep limbering up quietly. Don't fuss when you hear someone behind, and if they go past it means they're probably wearing themselves out early on. And don't forget that when you need it there's always a bit more in reserve, even if you think you can't go any faster. And, last bit of advice, when you're coming down, don't lose control. Do all those things and you'll win, and there'll be a couple of golden guineas from me, besides the cup." For the rest of the meal his father reminisced about the guide races he had run twenty years earlier. He did not usually talk so much. He was obviously nervous for his son.

Will's mother was unusually silent. She just watched Will eat his light meal, smiling encouragement once or twice while her husband talked on.

Vicky was waiting at the gate leading to the sports field with Tom's Elizabeth. Vicky was wearing her favorite tam-o'-shanter and a long green tweed coat and green gaiters against the cold. She was quiet, too. There was not very much to say. Will knew what was expected of him, and that second place would not do for her, and that she had absolute confidence that he could beat Buxton and all the other fast runners.

Tom joined them. He was running in the 100-yard sprint and had a good chance. They made small talk in a group, then Vicky pulled Will aside. "Give me your belt, Will," she whispered in his ear. "That's good luck, you know. I'll wear it while you're running, and I'll keep it forever if you win."

Will hoped that no one would notice as he unbuckled the leather belt. She rolled it deftly with her long fingers and slipped it in her handbag. "I'll get a seat as near the line as I can." The boys went off to the changing tent behind the main grandstand, and the girls were lost in the crowd.

For once it was a fine afternoon for the Amplethwaite Games. Held so late in the year, it was often rainy, and because it got dark early the program had to be run off rapidly. Some five thousand people had arrived from all over the district. Horses and ponies were tethered in a long line to hitching posts, and a corner of a field had been roped off for gigs, dogcarts, wagons, a dozen or more horse buses, and carriages belonging to the gentry. All along the side of the road were bicycles leaning against the stone wall and cars and motor buses from Workington, Barrow, Ulverstone, and other towns. Proudly in its customary place of honor against the church lych-gate stood the vicar's gleaming black Indian motor bicycle.

People were still arriving, and the motor bus from Windermere station deposited twenty more outside the main gate. This was Amplethwaite's great day of the year, and everything was being done in style. A brass band from Kendal was playing in the center of the arena, a dozen Union Jacks fluttered from flagpoles, and the church choir was lined up in readiness to offer the audience the traditional song of welcome. The only evidence of the war that had been raging across the Channel for more than two years was the splash of blue in the center of the main grandstand. The best seats had been reserved for the wounded servicemen from the nearby hospitals, and a number of those who could not walk were in wheelchairs on the grass in front.

During the afternoon, Will watched the events roll off one after the other—the wrestling, the boxing, the jumping, the weight lifting and javelin throwing, and the tumultuous release of first the puppies and then the hounds on their long trail across the fells. He was in a state of acute depression and uttered hardly a word. Why did everyone have to be so certain that he would win? This was his first year, he did not have the record of half the runners, his training had been brief. I was persuaded into it—I never wanted to, he told himself resentfully. And why do I have to be a winner? To come in the first ten wouldn't be bad.

He was cheered by the sight of Tom romping home in the 100 yards. He ran beautifully and never looked as though he were being challenged. There was a great cheer from the crowd for the local boy. Will cheered with the rest and got up to pat him on the back when Tom returned to his seat.

"Easy as eating pie," Tom said cheerfully. Will knew

that Tom had never doubted that he would win, and he wondered what it must be like to feel such marvelous self-confidence.

His depression set in again, and shortly before he was due to go out, Tom suddenly turned on him angrily. "You've been miserable company all afternoon," he said. "How do you expect to win with your face looking like that? The trouble with you, Will, is that you're too sorry for yourself. Self-pity, that's what they call it."

Will was so amazed to experience this attack by his old friend that he remained speechless for several seconds. Then he felt his own anger rising. What business was it of Tom's? He was still arguing hotly with Tom when the master of ceremonies bellowed through his megaphone: "Ladies and gentlemen—now we have the Junior Guide race for young gentlemen between fourteen and eighteen years."

Tom broke off the argument by saying, "Keep your steam up until the start. It'll help."

Will left his seat without a word. Twenty-nine other young men were making their way from the competitors' enclosure to the starting line in the center of the arena. None of them spoke, for the tension and the cold drove out all thought of communication.

Will was still seething with indignation. On his right, there was a farmer's boy from Langdale he knew by sight. He could not remember his name. A ridiculous-looking youth, like a spider, thought Will, with his long spindly legs and white arms. He had come in third or fourth last year and was tipped as a favorite. Will hated him. Then, there was Buxton—old lantern-jaw Buxton, strutting out as if he owned the place. Must be thirteen stone, and as unpleasant-looking an individual as you could imagine. Today, Will decided, he would beat Buxton—and all the rest of these spotty, swaggering young men.

There were three minutes remaining before the gun went off. Make your mind a blank, his father had advised, and much as Will had wanted to benefit from his father's experience, he found it impossible to escape from this feeling of anger at the whole world. He ran slowly up and down the track, raising his knees high and stretching his arms, his feet beating the turf in a vicious tattoo. Why was he so angry? he asked himself. He was hardly ever angry as a rule. Then a thought suddenly flashed to his mind: Tom had deliberately done this to him, to take his mind off his misery, and make him hate the other competitors. Clever old Tom! Will glanced at the competitors' stand. There was Tom, beside Will's empty seat. Will gave him a brief wave —and concentrated on his hate again.

The start of the guide race was always a shambles. There was no room for all the entrants to line up in a single row, and as the race was such a long one, it was no apparent disadvantage to be in the second row. But everyone knew what a help it was to have an unobstructed course and how it quelled your fighting spirit to see twenty or more figures ahead of you, splashing up the mud and getting in the way until you could pass them. The officials had always refused to bring any sort of order to the start, so it remained every man for himself. Will (the new, angry, ruthless Will) jostled his way into a good position in the front row, one away from Buxton, who had forced himself into the best center spot.

Will glanced to each side. He knew what he was going to do. He was going to start as if it were a 100-yard sprint. Above all, he must get clear of this mass of unpleasant humanity—break away and be free. Even if it meant overtaxing himself before the climb.

"On your mark . . ." The pistol cracked once, echoed from Amplethwaite Fell, and echoed distantly from the fell on the other side of the valley. By then they were all away, and Will could hear only the thunder of the footsteps on each side and behind him, and the sound of his own steady breathing. Will was a good sprinter, as he had shown Tom recently in the morning school dare. He had no difficulty in getting clear, and there was no one challenging him when he raced on to the first flagstones of the stone bridge. Ahead of him stretched the winding muddy path through the wood. It was marked with the innumerable paw marks of the hounds, which had earlier run howling along the same route on their aniseed-impregnated trail. If only he had their speed and stamina!

But Will was running very fast, avoiding the puddles from last night's rain and the worst patches of leaves. He was surprised when he heard someone come up beside him, and then saw him go ahead with a mighty sprint. It was a small lad from Grasmere who in practice had shown great eagerness but little staying power. Will knew that he was not a serious contender, but it was annoying to be led like this.

The challenge was brief. The Grasmere boy slipped on a damp patch just ahead and went sprawling. Will jumped neatly over him without breaking his pace, and in a dozen yards had leaped with two strides onto the top of the stone wall. It was good to be out of that damp wood, with the field and the fell rising open before him. He jumped from the top, landed in low, crisp bracken, and sped away across the sloping field toward the second wall. His legs felt fine, he was breathing well, and he was confident that no one could now take away his lead. At this stage, the triangular flag fluttering high above at the summit usually seemed almost unattainable. This evening it looked no distance away at all.

The lanky Langdale boy was the next runner to challenge Will. He came up alongside on one of the steepest parts, his spindly white arms driving hard against his spindly white legs, which were taking enormous strides upward. Will could not hope to hold this pace and watched him go by.

For fifty feet or so, you had to use your hands, and your speed depended a lot on your choice of route and selection of handholds. Will struggled to keep his head and avoid being fussed by the loss of the lead or by the pressure of twenty-eight more boys hard behind him. The rocks, the bunches of bracken or grass he clutched in turn, all held firm, and he made good time. Still only the spider was ahead. When he breasted this steep section, Will could see the spider had a huge lead and was already disappearing around the rocky summit, clapped on by a group of games' officials and a first-aid man.

Another runner had suddenly come alongside. Even before he turned for confirmation, Will was sure it was Buxton by his explosive breathing and his heavy presence. He could even smell the sweat of his body. His big jaw jutted forward in an attitude of relentless determination. Will felt the return of the rage that had burned in him at the start, and now it was concentrated on Buxton. He could not let this happen. He would not be overtaken by this coarse giant, and Will reached for the last of his reserve strength. At each upward step, he pressed hard with the palm of his hand against the top of his knee and for just long enough to feel the fiercely working muscles below the flesh. This was his limit, he could go no faster.

But Will's pace up that stretch of steep, rocky fell to the top was enough to stave off Buxton's challenge. Buxton never once got in front, and as they approached the pile of rock and the group of men beside it, Will was already three or four seconds ahead and gaining more time with every yard.

The leader had never reappeared from the far side of the summit. Will saw the reason as he rounded the flag. The Langdale boy had reached the top in record time and then collapsed under the strain. When Will went past, he was lying outstretched, more grotesquely spiderlike than ever in unconsciousness, with the first-aid man leaning over him.

A spasm of joy shot through Will. He was in the lead again. There was still a long fight ahead on the downward stretch, but he was bursting with self-confidence, and his legs felt strong, and his wind was holding up against the strain.

Before taking his first leap down, he caught a glimpse of the arena far below, an oval green patch finely marked with white lines, surrounded by the thick black lining of the crowd. Every face, Will knew, was turned toward the top of the fell, and the sharp-eyed among them would have seen his reappearance from the far side of the rocks—the leader was around the flag.

A cheer like the noise of waves on a distant pebble shore rose from the valley and reached Will's ears. Almost instantaneously, the noise of his own descent, the pounding of his feet on rock and dying bracken, and their skidding on a stretch of scree, overwhelmed all other sound. He shot like a projectile past the last runners still struggling to the top, spotted the rock that offered the great leap, stepped on it with his right foot, and launched himself off. He landed safely with bent knees among the bracken and sprang away without a pause and just before he heard the thud of Buxton landing a few feet behind. His lead was still desperately narrow, but he was holding it.

The ghyll had never given Will any trouble in practice.

You could take it in one leap at several places, and so long as you avoided the rocks strewn thickly on either side of its runnel, it did not delay you. Will saw its little falls shining in the last of the sunlight, like a diamond necklace dropped haphazardly down the fellside. He chose the same spot to jump it as he had in practice. But his takeoff was not clean. His left foot slipped slightly on the rock, and he landed on the other side off-balance.

At the speed he was traveling, the results of his misjudgment were multiplied many times over. His next step was wild, landing Will on a steeply sloping rock. An agonizing lance of pain shot up from his ankle. Now he was on boggy ground, and he skidded a couple of yards before losing all control and falling sideways. He rolled over and over a long way, striking several more rock outcrops before coming to rest spread-eagled on the ground.

Will cried out from the pain that pulsed in waves from a dozen cuts and bruises, and for a few seconds while he lay still with his eyes closed, the race was forgotten. The thud of footsteps close by brought him to his senses and to a consciousness of his responsibilities. It was Buxton, who had crossed the ghyll safely and was bounding heavily down the fellside in first place. As Will took his first step, he knew that he could never catch up with him. His left ankle, twisted and strained by that one false step, could hardly carry his weight. He limped for a dozen paces, his face drawn tight in agony, and fell again.

Twice more he tried. He could see the big figure far below, running faultlessly and with no one challenging him. Others were passing the spot where Will lay, more and more of them, a sweating, panting torrent of mud-splashed boys. Several of them glanced down at him, but there was no time or breath for a passing word of sympathy, and then the last of the strained faces was gone.

The first-aid man would soon come. It would be easy to yield to the temptation of the stretcher and the honorable carrying back to the arena. But Will was determined not to let this happen, and at least he must finish in his first Junior Guide. He hopped a few steps, tested his left ankle gingerly and discovered he could put some weight on it without too much pain, and began to hobble faster until he was traveling at a respectable speed. The ankle hurt, and so did two deep cuts in his right leg and the bruises and scratches on his right side. But at least he could get along, and he might even catch up with several of the tailenders. Several others had fallen, and the field was spread out over the lower half of the fell, with Buxton disappearing over the wall and into the wood. The sound of cheering was growing louder as Buxton approached the line.

Part of the crowd had surged into the arena, and their figures were tightly packed about the line. Dimly through eyes that were smarting from the pain and the sweat that poured from his forehead, Will could see that Buxton had already arrived and was surrounded by a group of his friends, and that half a dozen more were struggling for second place, each encouraged by the cheers of his supporters. The rest of the runners were still between Will and the line, their racing legs and straining backs forming a composite scene that sadly summarized the agony of the defeated athlete, the last in the race.

For Will, this moment and this spectacle formed the most humiliating experience of his life. If only there were some escape for him! But he was trapped into the funnel of this last stretch, the boy of promise who had not made good, his hobbling progress watched by thousands of eyes and accompanied by murmurs of sympathy that sounded like a dying motor, which cut off as he staggered over the last yards.

It rained on the day after the Amplethwaite Games, and on the succeeding six days too, with hardly a pause. The thunder of the swollen becks filled the valley, and the gray clouds swept in from the west on high fall winds like shore-bound rollers on a neap tide. It was cold and glum. In the evenings after school, Will spent most of his time in his room, in the cane bedside chair drawn up to the window, looking out. There was nothing to see. The fells were obscured down to five hundred feet, and the sweeping rain cut visibility to five hundred yards. Will's sense of failure was overwhelming, nor did it diminish with the passing days. It was accompanied by a gnawing sense of grief at the loss of Vicky. He might have been married to her for years, so appalling was the feeling of deprivation. If only he could be left in peace, he kept appealing to the rain-sodden skies. But of course life was a public business, at school and at home, when you were sixteen. There seemed to be no place of escape, except in his bedroom, and even here he hated his own company.

On the Sunday after the day of the games, Vicky's younger sister brought around a brown paper parcel and gave it to him without a word. It contained his belt—and a message in her round schoolgirl's writing: *I expected too much of you. After all, you're only a schoolboy. Sorry, V.* He knew it would happen, but the blow was no less savage for that.

Will spent most of the day with Dove, the strange old bachelor farmer up Russthwaite way, helping him with his sheep. They hardly exchanged two words, and Will found that peaceful and satisfactory.

His mother had seemed to take his defeat lightly. When he had first arrived home, she had been much more concerned about his ankle and cuts and bruises. "What a silly business this is, this stupid race. It's time it was stopped." She had knotted the last bandage tightly. "Now, how is that? You must go to bed and rest your leg now." That had been Saturday night. She had not said another word about his failure in the Junior Guide. But Will was certain that she secretly despised him for the poor performance that was in such marked contrast with the past triumphs of his father.

His father had tried to be kind, too, in his own silent way: only a few words of sympathy and encouragement. "You can't expect to learn it all first time, lad. I've had my own spills, you know."

The fall had been bad enough. It was an unforgivable piece of misjudgment, just when he was going so well and with every chance of winning. No, it was not really the fall. What Will knew, what he knew Vicky knew (and Tom and Elizabeth and all his friends and his mother and father) was that he could have won in spite of his loss of time and his injuries, or at least put up a manly struggle instead of just lying defeated on the fellside while Buxton romped away.

This was the accusation he kept hurling at himself, over and over again in the silence of his room. His courage had failed. He was a coward. Tom knew it. Tom had really meant it when he told Will before the start that he was self-pitying. Tom was right, as usual. Self-pity *was* cowardice. He had been running quite fast again and had hardly been limping at all at the end. Everyone must have noticed that. Coward and schoolboy. Vicky had used the word *schoolboy* as if it too was a term of abuse.

Between these self-accusations, Will relived those moments after the fall. Would it not have been better if he had never rejoined the race, had instead just lain among the rocks until he was helped to his feet? That would have seemed to the world a more honorable conclusion to his effort. But not to himself, of course. He could never have lived with the shameful and secret guilt this would have created.

And so the unhappy cycle of heart searching and sense of unworthiness raced around his mind until he fell wearily into bed.

Monday morning was the worst morning of Will's life. The whole village knew that Vicky had returned Will's leather belt, that the affair was over, that Will had made a poor showing in the Junior Guide. Will believed that most people would despise him and only a few would be sympathetic. He dreaded more the words of sympathy. The school cloakroom was packed with dripping wet boys struggling out of their raincoats and changing out of their boots. They were all talking about the games, some shouting to make themselves heard above the echoing voices of the others. As Will walked through the wet, jostling crowd toward his peg, the sound of the voices diminished about him, and curious faces turned in his direction. There was a snicker from a junior boy, followed by a brief scuffle. A fourteen-year-old bent over his locker murmured, "Rotten luck on Saturday, Will."

Will knew what they were all thinking, for there was a great school loyalty at Amplethwaite Private, enthusiastically encouraged by the Venners. Everyone knew that, for the first time ever, the school could have won the Junior Guide; the silver cup could this morning have been sitting proudly with the others on the dining room mantelpiece, the subject of a few fulsome words of praise from Mr. Venner at Prayers. Instead it had gone to that muscular dockyard worker, Buxton.

Thank goodness for Tom! He was marvelous. He passed off the whole affair lightly and briskly devised a conversation distraction. In *Boy's Own Paper* he had found plans and instructions on how to make a model airplane. It was the first time either of them had seen anything like it. Before the bell rang for the school roster, Tom had already shown the magazine to Will, and during midmorning recess they sat together in a corner of the school hall with the rain beating on the windows, studying the plans in detail. It was one of the scouts Hugh Sanderson had flown before his squadron had converted to Pups. When Will told him, Tom said at once, "Let's make it for him, then. It'll cheer him up in hospital."

At first this seemed to Will a marvelous idea. Then he realized that he would never again visit the pilot. How could he ever explain his failure? "I had a bit of a fall—strained my ankle—came in last . . ." No, that was quite impossible.

Tom was saying, "I've got the right sort of wood, and we can buy some of that twine we'll need for the bracing wires . . ."

They would build it anyway, and Will would send it to Hugh Sanderson. It would be something to do during these long, damp evenings and would stop him from brooding and thinking about Vicky.

But the feeling of utter defeat and depression overwhelmed Will again at the end of the day. By five o'clock, the rain had turned to a light drizzle, and the usual jostling, chattering crowd had assembled about the school gates. All day Will had managed to avoid looking for Vicky. But now the sight of her sitting on the wall and drumming her heels against the stones as if the world were an unchanged place sent a shock of pain through him. He tried to hurry past, but two juniors obstructed his path. They looked up when he tried to get by. "Do you need carrying home, then?"

one of them asked cheekily and then dodged away laughing, as if expecting a blow.

Tom came around to Will's house later in the evening and said they could not start on the model that night, as Elizabeth wanted to go roller-skating in Kendal and his father had told him he could borrow the dogcart. The black day closed about Will when he heard this news. Tom had brought around the copy of *Boy's Own Paper* and some wood. "You make a start on the wings tonight," he suggested cheerfully, "and we'll work on it together tomorrow."

When the door closed behind Tom, Will let the magazine fall onto the kitchen table. It landed beside his father's newspaper. NEW ATTACK ON THE SOMME ran the headline. GERMANS FALL BACK AND SUFFER HEAVY LOSSES. Will's eyes turned from the magazine to the newspaper and back again, and he was suddenly struck by the contrast between the two worlds they represented. There, ready for his father when he came in from the bakery, was the news of the real world, the men's world, in which soldiers—like Hugh Sanderson—were fighting desperately for their country. He picked up the B.O.P., as they all called it. Stories, serials, nature tips, and how to make a model airplane. This was still his world.

His mother came bustling in with a basket of eggs. "It's coming down harder than ever," she said cheerfully. "Fine weather for ducks, but the hens don't like it." She shook out her coat. "Help me set the table, love."

On November 27, 1916, Will Thompson left his home and his mother and father and the village of Amplethwaite; left the Amplethwaite Private School and Mr. and Mrs. Venner; Tom Filton and his girl, Elizabeth; his other friends; and lovely Vicky, who cared for him no longer. He left behind him the stone walls and fells, the turning bracken, the running becks, the winding tracks and lanes of Westmorland; and in his room a pile of school books and notebooks, and a half-completed model airplane.

Will told no one. He hid his bicycle and a pack containing some clothes and a letter behind a wall on the way to school in the morning. In the evening after school, he retrieved his bicycle and pedaled off for Windermere station. No one saw him go, no one at Windermere questioned him. He bought a single ticket on the night train to London from his £4 savings and settled back in his seat for the long journey.

Will was still dazed by the pace and turn of events of his

life, and confused by the conflict of emotions created by the wonder at his own vigor and decisiveness and the guilt for his secretiveness. His parents would be alarmed by his disappearance, and his mother would be distraught when she heard that he had joined up. Perhaps his father would be proud. Will was not sure. But he planned to write to them after he arrived in London, to tell them what he intended to do and to reassure them that he was well.

Will's success in the enterprise that lay ahead depended, he knew, on his own endurance, determination, and courage. He would show himself that he still had these qualities. In the past two weeks, he had thought about things with care and clarity. He was certain that he was doing the right thing. The gray world between youth and manhood was no place for him any longer. He had for too long been fed up with himself, with the anguish and humiliation of being the loser—whether of a race or of his girl. On the one side of his gray world was self-pity, on the other self-respect. Anger had at last driven him out. At the same time, he knew that the departure itself was nothing. Anyone could mount a bicycle and buy a ticket at the station. The testing time lay ahead—when he arrived in London alone with few possessions, little money, and the letter. If the letter failed, then he would simply go to the nearest recruiting station and join an infantry regiment—any regiment, it did not matter. But he would not return.

The letter in his pocket was from Lieutenant Hugh Sanderson, M.C., R.F.C., from the military convalescent hospital near London to which he had been sent from Preston. There were no jokes in it. It was a brisk and businesslike answer to Will's request for help to get into the Royal Flying Corps.

Yes, he had written, *I'll do my best to help you. You should make a good pilot. Come and see me after your eighteenth birthday, and I'll have a word with someone who may get you in.* And after he had finished his training, Will had been told, he should try to get a posting to his own squadron. *By the time you've finished your training, I'll be back with my flight,* Sanderson had ended his letter, *and you can help watch my tail.*

When Will had received this letter in answer to his own, all work with Tom on the model plane had ceased. Behind the words, he could hear the crisp voice of Sanderson and the sound of a real plane—a Sopwith Pup—roaring across the sky. As to his age—well, there was still a year and a bit before he was eighteen, but to cheat over your age was not regarded as dishonest. You were a brave fellow, and good luck to you if you could get away with it. That was the popular view.

Will was awakened from a restless doze in the early hours of the morning by the sound of gunfire. Momentarily his confused dreams were reshaped to real war, and he was already at his airfield on the western front. His eyes opened to darkness. The carriage lights had been switched off, and the train was stationary. Two passengers were leaning out of the open window staring up at the sky. "They've caught him," one of them was saying excitedly. Will looked up through the window into the night sky. There, thousands of feet above and shining like a long silver bar in the light of searchlight beams, was a Zeppelin. The Midlands was being raided. Will would never forget these first sounds and sights of war: the long yellow fingers of the searchlight beams crisscrossing the sky, the spread and instantaneous disappearance of the sparkles of antiaircraft fire, the ear-splitting *crack-crack-crack* of a nearby gun battery, the muzzle flashes spreading sudden white light across houses and streets, and the distant repeated *c-r-u-m-p* of exploding bombs.

"They've caught him all right," repeated one of the

passengers. "Now you watch, it'll burst into flames in a minute."

Will could imagine the German Zeppelin crew at their stations in their airship. It would be bitterly cold up there at about fifteen thousand feet, with the darkened towns spread out beneath them, and with the certain knowledge that one hit might detonate the great volume of hydrogen that alone kept them afloat in the sky. Only a few weeks before, Will had read how one of these giant ships of the sky had fallen in flames after being shot down by a scout—and no one had escaped alive from the holocaust.

Between the crack of the guns and the spasmodic thunder of exploding bombs, he could hear the distant drone of scout engines struggling to gain equal altitude with the Zeppelin and to bring their gunsights to bear on their target. And in his imagination he moved to the scout's cockpit, with the throttle open wide, the night air rushing past, and, growing ever nearer above him, the giant target with its gunners waiting tensely for him to come within range. . . .

What a night to travel to London, and to go off to the war! Will stared in fascination as the lumbering craft disappeared into the distance, swallowed up by clouds, and the sounds of battle faded into the distance. The passengers collapsed back into their seats, and the train jerked again into movement. In another two hours, they would be in London.

Even at four o'clock in the morning, the big mainline station was busy with the traffic of war and echoed to the crack of steel-heeled boots. Will sat down and then fell off to sleep on a wooden bench half-filled with slumped figures in khaki, clutching rifles and duffel bags. Soon after six o'clock and while it was still dark, he made his way out of the station and ate breakfast in a cheap café. Everyone was talking about the Zeppelin raid. Bombs had fallen on many parts of the north of England and the Midlands. People had been killed, but two of the raiders had been shot down.

Will arrived at the army convalescent home in the suburbs of London early in the afternoon. It was a crisp, clear winter day. The Georgian mansion and its beautiful grounds had been taken over by the military. Now officers with shattered limbs or blinded by gas or shell blast sat, well wrapped, in wheelchairs on the terraces where rich and elegant people had once strolled, chatting and admiring the gardens. He found Hugh Sanderson without difficulty. He was sitting fretfully in one of the wheelchairs, talking to his neighbors and throwing gravel at a sundial. The pilot greeted Will warmly and demanded that he should push him—fast—up and down the terrace. "It makes me feel I'm getting some exercise," he said. "And, talking of exercise, how did the race go?"

Will began hesitantly. "Well, I . . ."

Then, to Will's consternation, the pilot broke into laughter. "So you didn't! So what? Nothing to be ashamed about. You can't always win, you know. Look at me with this leg. You can't say I was a winner that time. Now, one more lap —only faster . . ."

When Hugh Sanderson called a halt, Will was panting and couldn't at once reply to the question, "What brings you here?"

"You said you would help me get into the R.F.C. That's why I've come to London."

"So you're eighteen, are you?" Hugh Sanderson turned his head and smiled conspiratorially. "But you've got to understand that you're probably signing your own death warrant. About five weeks is the average."

"Average what?"

Hugh Sanderson laughed loudly. "Average expectation of life. That's what they say, anyway. I'm just a statistical freak. Mark you, the new bus is a great improvement. Helps your chances."

"Have you had any news from your squadron?"

"They're all mad about the Pup. Very maneuverable, they say. Can turn twice inside an Albatros. And they like the speed, 110 miles an hour, and you can push them up to 160 in a dive." He felt clumsily with his gloved hand for an inside pocket beneath his overcoat and pulled out a letter. " 'We got four Albatroses and three Fokkers in the last four days,' " he read aloud. " 'Not bad, but we need you back for decent scores. Charlie Moore was shot down behind the lines last week—he may be a prisoner—and we lost two new pilots last week. The first month's the worst, they say. Lots of dud weather, but we've got a big show this afternoon. . . .' And then he goes on about parties and things. Some of the chaps threaten to invade this place this afternoon."

Will was fascinated. This was the real war in the air, not romanticized for the magazines and full of heroics. A chill of dread combined with excited expectation seized hold of him, and he wanted to talk all day with Sanderson about his squadron and the fighting on the western front.

Instead Sanderson talked about training. "They'll give you a couple of months of square-bashing first. The idea is that they have to make a soldier of you: 'Present a-r-m-s. Eyes r-i-g-h-t.' All that sort of thing," said Sanderson, mockingly carrying out these orders from the confines of his chair. "Then, if you're no good at flying, they can put you in the trenches as cannon fodder. Then for another two months you'll do schoolwork: How does a rotary engine rotate, how to fly from here to there when there's a wind blowing at twenty miles an hour from 270 degrees, what is a Vickers gun, and how to clear a stoppage. You'll be called an officer cadet, and you'll be the lowest form of human life, practically vermin."

Was he never going to fly? wondered Will. It would be months before he would be in the air at this rate.

"If you get through that, then you'll get some leave and you'll wait for a posting to a reserve squadron for initial training," Sanderson went on. "Then it'll be Maurice Farmans—if you think *those* are airplanes, you'll need your head examined. But the day will come"—and he accelerated his chair forward to a fast walking pace—"when you'll leave the ground at about this speed and somehow stagger up all by yourself. And you'll be frightened stiff." He laughed so loudly that a nurse hurrying nearby turned sharply in alarm. "I'll never forget the first time I soloed. I took the top branches off a tree, flopped around like a drunken sea gull for five minutes, and dropped back to earth and took off the undercarriage."

Hugh Sanderson held the wheels of the chair to draw it to a halt and looked around at Will. There was for the first time an expression of seriousness on his young, freckled, battered face. "If you're serious and really want to go through all this, I'll write a letter to Derek Barber. If anybody can pull this off, he will. Major Barber is head of the Postings and Recruitment branch at the War Office in Whitehall. I'll mail it today, and you go and see him tomorrow. He's an old friend of mine, but you'll find him sticky going. He likes to pretend he's tough, and he'll try to frighten you. But if you can win him over, you'll be all right."

The officers Sanderson had expected arrived in a staff car. There were three of them, fellow pilots on leave from the squadron and in high spirits. Sanderson swung his chair in their direction and pushed off at speed to meet them. Will listened to the hearty greetings and the loud exchange of banter and wondered if he could ever play a part in this easygoing man's world of courage and shoptalk and total self-confidence. He wanted to slip away unseen, but Sanderson spotted him making for the hospital gates and called out for him to come back.

"I want you to meet this budding flier," he told his friends. "He dragged me out of some wild mountain torrent and saved my life. Then he ran like a Fokker in a power dive for help. These are three survivors of the Somme holocaust, Will, not that they deserve to live, considering how rottenly they flew. Lieutenant Algernon Black, Lieutenant Rodney Strangeways, and Captain Cyril Horne—note the captain. Got your three pips last week, didn't you, Shoehorn?"

Will shook each strong hand solemnly in turn. He knew he ought to be putting on a good show, but he could not think what to say. "I hope to join your squadron soon, sir," he said to the captain. "The Pup looks like a marvelous airplane."

He left the three pilots pushing Sanderson up and down the lawn, talking shop and laughing. They were enjoying themselves hugely, and the war seemed to them to be as much fun as a long and fierce game of rugby.

The major could not see him for half an hour. It had taken all Will's resolution to get as far as a waiting room in the War Office. He had felt overwhelmed and hopelessly inadequate at the War Office entrance among the purposeful figures that marched in and out, saluting and giving crisp orders. One red-tabbed officer, his breast blazing with decorations, had given him a passing glance. It was the only notice taken of him until he forced himself to approach a sergeant at one of the doors. "You want the recruiting office," he was told; and it was some minutes before he could regain the sergeant's attention. "Major Barber? Major Barber? He won't be able to see you."

But he was. He would see Will in half an hour. And meanwhile Will could look out of the deep windows from which, above the pile of protective sandbags, he could see the overwhelming skyline of London, the greatest city in the world. It was the first time that he had been here, and it was bigger and stranger than he had ever imagined it would be.

Will was escorted to the major and received in absolute silence, greeted by no more than a nod toward a chair before his desk. There was a clock against one wall, and it ticked the seconds away solemnly while Major Barber read twice through the letter he had received from Hugh Sanderson. At last he swung around his swivel chair and glared at Will. He was a formidable-looking figure with a quite circular red face, scarred by a terrible burn wound on the left cheek. Below the major's wings, Will recognized the ribbons of the D.S.O. and Croix-de-Guerre. The major stood up, grabbed the stick that had been hanging from the side of his desk, and limped up and down as he talked.

"So young Hugh thinks you'll make a pilot. Why does he think that?" The words sounded like shots from a Vickers machine gun.

Will knew that his answer might settle his future. He was sitting bolt upright in the chair, his mind alertly hunting for the right answer.

"I think he thought I was keen, sir. I talked to him when he was in hospital near where I live. I told him I wanted to fly."

"A lot of people want to fly. But can they, eh?"

"I'm sure I will be able to, sir." He wondered if he should go on. But the major was still glaring at him as if he had not yet received a satisfactory answer. "And I can shoot quite well."

"You mean grouse and deer, I suppose."

"Well, rabbits, sir. I am quite a good shot." He paused uncertainly again, then decided to take a chance and recount the shooting episode in the hospital. He had no encouragement from his audience, and he found it hard to tell the story in proper sequence. Before he had reached the end, the interview took a startling new turn.

"You mean to say Hugh had set up his own firing range?" The major burst into bellows of laughter and had to sit down heavily in his seat. "Good old Hugh. What a lad! But just like him. In dud weather he used to line up six glasses along the bar and didn't allow himself a drink until he had smashed them all with his .38 revolver—lying flat on the floor. Very, very illegal. Nobody else could get a drink either, so we used to cheer him on." He swung around on Will again. "Well, what did you do?" he snapped.

"I hit one of the targets he kept missing."

Will had broken through, and the major was all smiles and helpfulness now. He looked at the letter again. It was very irregular, he said. Most pilots had already seen some war in another arm of the service, from which they transferred. But he would do what he could, for old Hugh's sake. And if old Hugh had backed the wrong horse, he, Major Barber, would take Hugh off scouts and put him on instructing. That would teach the old devil.

The interview took another turn. It seemed suddenly to be over, for the major was taking no more interest in him and was giving his attention instead to some papers on his desk. Will got up to go. "Where shall I report, sir?"

"Report? Oh, they'll tell you outside. By the way," he continued with renewed interest, "how old are you?"

"Eighteen." Will was ready for that.

"You'll need your father's consent. Any trouble there?"

Will was quite unprepared for this and was so taken aback that he hardly heard himself tell his second thundering lie. "He's dead, sir. So is my mother."

This exasperated the major. "Oh, great Scot! What a morning you're giving me! All right, you're eighteen, you want to join the flying corps, you haven't any parents, you haven't even got a guardian. More red tape to smash up." He scribbled a note and handed it to Will. "If you've got a name, give it to the sergeant outside. A new course starts at Oxford in a day or two. If you're passed fit, you'll be in that." He lowered his scarred head to his desk. There was no more to be said.

Will was buoyed up by his success with the major and, the next day, by his medical examination, which he passed A1. He had no time to be bored and lonely. With the completion of his tests, he had only a few hours in his rented room before he was due to set off for Oxford for his initial training. He filled this time by writing a long letter to his mother and father, asking forgiveness for leaving without their permission and without saying good-bye. *I hope you will understand . . .* he wrote, and he felt that his mother would. And that she would understand the P.S. he added at the end: *I'd like to write to Vicky, but I don't think she would want me to.* He also wrote to Tom and—rather to his own surprise—to Mr. and Mrs. Venner, apologizing for leaving school in the middle of the term without authority. He had a feeling that they might not disapprove of his decision—the Venners were very patriotic, called Germans the Boche, and were quite bloodthirsty about them.

It was a cold, hard winter, which later left in Will's memory a multitude of sounds and sights: of the sharply exhaled clouds of breath from the sergeant-major's mouth when he barked orders; of the metallic crash of fifty heels stamping against the stone of the square; of the bells of Oxford ringing out in uneasy accompaniment to his striding steps; of voices echoing in the hall when they assembled for tea after a long day of drill and gym and instruction; of the newspaper boys crying the latest war headlines in the High.

It was a strange time of change and adjustment. On the one hand, Will felt deeply the loss of freedom and, on the other hand, a relief from the responsibility of decision. Every moment of every day was filled for him as his mind and body were efficiently reshaped for the needs of war. He was asked only to respond to the simple orders of the corporal or sergeant-major. These two fierce men treated the recruits uniformly as if they were simpletons who, for their own good, must be firmly handled. An officer who had been gassed a year earlier and looked as if he might die at any time irritably instructed them in the fundamentals of military law and custom. A pilot with six months of fighting behind him gave them a lecture on the art of aerial warfare. Every day there was a new face, a new experience. Sometimes late at night lying in his narrow, hard bed, Will wondered at the contrast between the comfortable predictability of his old life in Amplethwaite and the harsh rituals and unfamiliar scenes of military training in this city. But he was too tired to give it much thought, and he soon learned to stem the tide of the memories of Vicky and the loneliness and homesickness that still threatened to flood into his mind in the rare moments when he was alone.

Through the arduous, cold winter weeks, he was supported by the presence, day and night, of the other officer cadets in the course, who shared the rigors and grumbled in unison and laughed at one another, the eccentricities of the major, and even the fearful food. Within a few days after they had gathered at the Oxford headquarters, untidy and unmilitary in their civilian clothes, they had become a unit of familiar faces in identical khaki uniforms. Some were self-confident from the start and with the seeds of excellence, some reserved and cautious, some foul-mouthed, a few were intellectuals who sought quickly their own kind, and a few more carried the mark of failure. Class divisions cut them into groups. A dozen upper-class private schoolboys held themselves together, but not so tightly as three who were evidently newly rich—the sons of industrialists who were doing well from the war. Will slipped easily into the lowest and largest stratum of middle-class shopkeepers, young men he could talk to without restraint. Nobody worried about the divisions. They had known them all their lives and found them simple and satisfactory, and their uniform and their training held them together loyally as a unit; and no one wearing a cadet's uniform—the symbol of lowest status—could get above himself for long.

They lived in an Oxford college close by other colleges whose scholarly timelessness contrasted oddly with their own noisy preparation for the brief predatoriness of war, and made the barked orders of their instructors sound profane. The eternal studies, Will suddenly realized when he was fixing his bayonet one morning, would still be continuing when he and all his fellow cadets were going about their noisy, bloody business in a few months' time.

There was always a good deal of the threatening and menacing talk in which all young warriors have indulged since the time of the Trojan wars, in order to steel themselves for combat and to convince themselves and their fellows of their courage.

The most belligerent boy in the course was called Fred Turner. He was the son of a factory department supervisor in South Shields, with red hair and a ruddy complexion toughened by nineteen years of North Sea east wind. His conversation was so unremittingly fierce that no one could hope to match it, and after a while people began to flinch away from it. This only made Turner work harder at being the tough nut. "There's a lot of stupid talk about taking prisoners," he would say, accusingly and in his broad Northumberland accent. "Well, I'll tell you, I'm not taking any. War's war, and you're there to kill your enemy, not arrest him like some soft policeman."

One Saturday night, Turner got very drunk on beer, came in late, and knocked over the corporal on guard. The guard had been prepared to let him in quietly, but this was not good enough for Turner: He had to show what a man he was by picking a quarrel and punching the innocent fellow. Turner at bayonet drill after being reprimanded by the commanding officer was the ugliest sight Will had ever seen. He tore the sack dummy to shreds with a dozen terrible slashes and came back to the rank foaming at the mouth. Heaven help the Germans when Turner gets to the front, Will thought.

There were other memorable faces in the square-bashing course, and others in the technical and theoretical course that followed it and lasted eight weeks, but the heavy figure of Fred Turner with his big stubby hands and ferocious demeanor stood out above all the others.

No one made any close friends. There was no time, and they knew that, whether they failed or succeeded, they would be split up at the end. And what they were all really waiting for was the start of flight training. The marching and bayoneting, the rifle shooting and presenting of arms, then the air navigation and map reading, the study of aero engines and airframes—all were regarded as necessary but dull preliminaries to taking off and soaring into the sky.

Will left Oxford in early March 1917, the single pip of a second lieutenant on his shoulders, a silk-lined khaki uniform of wonderful smoothness and comfort after the harsh serge he had worn as a cadet, a stick, soft leather gloves, and a certificate to show that he had passed honorably with a grade of 70 percent and was fit to begin flight training. He had four days' leave before going to his reserve squadron. Should he go home? He had the money to travel now, and he ached for a sight of the fells, after the flatness of the southern landscape, and the sound of the becks, the scent of the log fire at home; and he would have enjoyed showing off his uniform to his friends—those mere schoolchildren.

To his surprise, he found himself asking the advice of another new young officer in his course, a crisp, tight little fellow with a freckled face called Haddow, who had done six months in the trenches before transferring to the R.F.C. and seemed like a worldly-wise veteran. Haddow knew that Will had put up his age to get in and told him firmly not to go near his village until he had completed his training. "Some old busybody is bound to tell—probably the verger or the secretary of the Woman's Institute or some worm at your school who's jealous of your new manliness." He had laughed and told Will to come and stay with him instead.

In the end, it was the thought of seeing Vicky that deterred Will. He longed to glimpse again her hair and her face and her hands and to see her walking very straight and trim down the Amplethwaite street. But he wanted to have more than the fresh uniform of a junior second lieutenant when next they met. For his own pride and self-esteem, he needed to have accomplishment behind him. In a weak moment of which he was immediately ashamed, he imagined the terse announcement in the Westmorland *Gazette* of his Military Cross.

So he had written a long letter to his parents instead, to ease his conscience, and spent the brief leave in Haddow's modest house in an East Anglia village, accustoming himself to his new status and going for long walks in the rain and listening to Haddow's tales of his life in the trenches. The reality of war became much nearer, and his own past life as a schoolboy in Amplethwaite more remote. "I feel in a sort of limbo, neither one thing nor the other," he once confessed to Haddow, who was a relaxing and easy person to talk to. "It'll be different when you get in the air," he had replied. "That'll be the real thing, and you won't have any time to brood."

"It's different for you. You've fought already. You've killed Germans and know what it's all about."

Wise Haddow answered, "Different, yes. But the one thing I've learned about this war is that you don't count a damn. You're like a mass-produced Ford car, and things happen to you. Somebody puts a body on to you like this idiot uniform, and then someone makes sure your engine works all right, and then you're sold off to someone who either drives you hard into a brick wall or works you until you're no good and you're sent on leave for an overhaul. That's what it was like in the trenches, and I expect it'll be the same in the R.F.C. All this stuff about intrepid birdmen rushing around the sky looking for Huns to shoot down is all my eye. We'll be in squadrons, probably with an inefficient idiot commanding officer who'll tell us just what to do. And we'll be killed looking after his rotten tail."

Will was both shocked and impressed by this outburst. But he was to remember it again, many times.

"The Rumpty," said Lieutenant Henry Nicholls, R.F.C. with absolute authority, "is a bastard. A bastard to look at, a bastard to climb into, a bastard to start, and a bastard to fly. It is my unfortunate task, gentlemen, to teach you to fly her."

His head turned from one to the other of his four pupil pilots and then to the curious assemblage of bracing wires, struts, and doped canvas surfaces of the Farman Shorthorn, or Rumpty, trainer airplane. "You may well look dubious, gentlemen, and you would be correct in your surmise that aeronautical development has not moved one inch since the Wright brothers first went aloft nearly fourteen years ago. But you are going to fly that birdcage, or break your neck in the process. Probably the latter."

It was a sunny day in early April. The wind was too cold to let you think about spring, and Will, frozen in his heavy greatcoat, wondered how their instructor, in old stained tunic and battered breeches, could stand it. He had a wiry frame and a lurching manner of walking caused by shrapnel wounds in his left leg. After only twenty-four hours at Ledslade airfield, Will had learned that he was the most fearsome and efficient instructor at this station; that his pupils soloed in the shortest time; that he had done 150 missions as a scout pilot, been shot down four times by German planes and once by antiaircraft fire, and had five Fokkers, an Aviatik, and three balloons to his credit.

"Lieutenant Nicholls don't stand no nonsense, sir," the barman had told Will on his first evening. Will recognized the truth of this within minutes of being summoned to his office. Nicholls, Will discovered, had transferred from his infantry regiment before the end of 1914, when he thought it would be a long, static war, a muddy war, not the sort of war he was likely to enjoy. The R.F.C. looked more promising. He had survived eighteen months of flying, all on the western front, and that was something of a record. He had the Military Cross ribbon on his left breast beneath his wings, and even these wings appeared to need cleaning. Everything about him was dirty, and Will was soon to become familiar with his smell of sweat, grease, and castor oil. He had a narrow, angry face, already deeply lined at twenty-four-or-so years, and a black toothbrush mustache. He was an unprepossessing-looking man. But he had about him the special quality of the veteran warrior and a sense of fearless self-confidence that was reassuring. Will was prepared to idolize him.

Lieutenant Nicholls took his party of raw pupils around the machine, pointing out the rudder, the elevator, and the ailerons and the function and operation of these three basic airplane controls. They climbed in turn up onto the step of the forward nacelle and peered down into the two diminutive cockpits, one behind the other. The simple controls and instruments were placed just as they had been taught during their training: The rudder bar, the joystick, the throttle lever in its quadrant, the instruments, even the little curved windshield—were all as Will knew they would be. He had seen this a hundred times in diagrams and drawings in the textbooks he had been studying. Now he was looking at the real thing. Tomorrow, or even today, he, William Thompson of Amplethwaite, Westmorland, ex-schoolboy, age sixteen years nine months, would be sitting in that cockpit, working those controls—flying!

Lieutenant Nicholls was continuing his mordant introduction to the Rumpty. "One other thing about the curious design of this flying machine," he was saying, his stick resting on one of the propeller blades. "With the engine behind your head, when you come to a sudden halt, like hitting something, if you don't kill yourself against what you hit, you can rely on this engine to finish you off from behind. The Rumpty is a merciful machine. She leaves few wounded survivors."

Will was missing nothing. He listened carefully to Nicholls' every word. But the most vehement criticism of the Rumpty could not destroy his sense of reverence toward this birdcage machine. It was only an antiquated trainer. He had to share it with three others. It might kill one of them. But it was his first machine—*his* own bus.

The inspection was over. Lieutenant Nicholls stood with his hands on his hips and his head on one side, staring at the machine like a schoolmaster considering a recalcitrant child. "Well, that's it, gentlemen. To look at her, you wouldn't believe she can fly, but it's my business to show you that she can just be made to lift herself off the ground —and then it'll be your turn." He looked up at the scattered scudding clouds. "But not today. The Rumpty does not care for gusty winds, or any wind at all, for she is not a strong creature. So we shall return for some theory."

They walked together in a group behind the limping figure, back across the grass to the wooden hut containing the instructors' offices and the lecture hall. All around were the sights and sounds and smells of airfield life, which were already becoming a part of Will's life. The wind sock was full-blown and quivering in the wind, and the sound of two engines being tested and running at high revs thundered out from a nearby hangar. Riggers were working on several of the planes lined up neatly at the edge of the field. There was the ambulance, the busiest machine on the airfield, Nicholls had told them with relish; and fuel and maintenance trucks were going about their business. Close to the hangar's open doors, Will caught a whiff of the sharp evocative smell of pure castor oil. Above them, an Avro was flying low and crosswind, crabbing at an acute angle. When the pilot turned downwind, the machine seemed to be hurled across the sky at an unnatural speed. Then the pilot turned on the last leg, lowered the Avro's nose, and came down lower and lower, holding off just above the grass while the last of her speed fell away and dropping neatly onto her two wheels and tail skid.

All this was the special private world of the airfield. And now Will was part of it.

Lieutenant Nicholls was wrong about the weather. After lunch, the wind dropped. At two o'clock, the major went up to smell the air, did a quick circuit, and landed and told the instructors that flying could begin. One by one, propellers were swung into life, and soon the air was filled with the roar of a half-dozen Rumpty engines, and Nicholls had to shout to make himself heard. "This is the only time you'll fly and have nothing to do," he told his group. "It's a joy-ride—familiarization, we call it. If you're sick, put your head well out. Come on, Jones, I'll have you." He nodded at the tallest of them, a silent lad from south London who seemed to carry in his lanky body few seeds of the warrior.

Without apparent order, the Rumptys taxied out clumsily across the grass, each with its eager pupil pilot in new flying gear sitting in the plane's nacelle, the instructor handling the controls.

Will watched their plane jog across the grass and turn into the wind, the figure of Jones like some ridiculous stump mast in the nose, his head high above the windshield. He wondered how Jones was feeling as a helpless victim, for there was no turning back now.

Jones survived the ordeal creditably, and there was a slight swagger in his gait as he stepped away from the Rumpty and rejoined them twenty minutes later. "I don't think I'll have much trouble handling that bus," he remarked surprisingly. A new Jones seemed already to have been born.

Will was next. Nicholls remained in the cockpit with the engine still *put-put-putter*ing away behind him, shaking the Rumpty's frame. He gave no instructions except to shout, "Keep the strap tight, it's bumpy." And before Will had settled, the note of the engine rose and they were moving away toward the field's boundary fence. There were two more Rumptys already there waiting to take off, and a group of boys leaning on their bicycles was watching them from the road. There was a woman with a baby carriage, too. She waved to Will, and he began to raise his arm in cheerful reply, then remembered his dignity and that he was now a man in a man's world. He was sorry later, for she had meant well.

Everything about the next ten minutes was unexpected. During the months he had dreamed of flying, he had imagined himself with stout wings at each side and above him, a whirling propeller in front. He had expected to be filled with an acute sense of excitement and speed, and to see the world float away beneath him as he soared upward. For Will, flying was diving and climbing and banking steeply among the fells in a Sopwith Pup, turning suddenly to fire off a burst of machine-gun fire—dead on target.

The reality of that first flight was very different. At first, it was like freewheeling down a bumpy hill on a bicycle. There was none of the feeling of speed he had once experienced on the pillion of the vicar's Indian motor bicycle, and Will felt that he did not need the protection of his goggles. At about thirty miles an hour, the bumping of the wheels diminished and then stopped altogether. Will looked down and was curious to see that the grass was a few feet below. He was flying.

It seemed to take a long time to reach the far end of the field. There were two men digging ditches in the next field. They did not even look up, which offended him. Didn't they realize that he was flying? The tops of the trees ahead were higher than the airplane, but it was still climbing, steadily if slowly. They cleared the trees easily, and Will saw rooks building their big careless nests. They were no more interested in the Rumpty than the laborers had been.

The altimeter needle showed four hundred feet. This was as high as they would go, Nicholls had told them. At Amplethwaite he could climb higher than this in a few minutes on his own feet. But here in this frail cockpit, there was no hard granite under his feet, and only the lift provided by two improbably frail wings and the spinning propeller behind held him from plunging into the dizzy gulf below.

The Rumpty was bouncing about heavily, and Will could see reproduced in the dual controls in front of him the correcting movements of joystick and rudder that Nicholls was making. Suddenly the stick was moved far to the left, the right wings went sharply up, and the horizon swung correspondingly as the airplane went into a banked turn. It was gentle enough but felt like the first plunge toward annihilation. Will clutched tightly at the edge of the cockpit and prayed for the return of equilibrium. Up went one end of the horizon and down the other until it was again level. They had reversed course. Ahead and below was the airfield dotted with the shapes of parked and taxiing airplanes. A machine was taking off, and as it climbed it separated itself from its shadow and left it far behind. With the wind behind them, they seemed to be traveling at twice their earlier speed. Then Nicholls pulled back the throttle and cut the engine. They fell fast with the sound of the wind whistling in the bracing wires.

"This is quite safe if you keep the needle above forty-five miles an hour." Nicholls' voice was at its normal volume, as if they were talking on the ground. The grass came up to meet Will at an alarming speed. They seemed certain to plunge into it. And yet the voice continued to talk quite calmly, as if this was to be a normal landing instead of a disastrous nosedive. Will was puzzled that Nicholls should be facing destruction of plane, pupil, and himself so calmly. He put his arm protectively over his face at the same moment that the engine burst into life again. He felt his body being pressed against the cane seat, and when he looked again, the Rumpty was floating with marvelous steadiness a few feet above the ground, with the engine just ticking over. The wheels nudged the ground gently, and they settled into a perfect three-point landing.

Lieutenant Nicholls was tying up his bootlace when Will climbed down from the cockpit. He did not even look up.

"Let's have the next one, and tell him to hurry up. I'm getting a sore arse." It all seemed oddly matter-of-fact after what they had been through. Will decided that flying, so far, was unexpected in every way. Not disappointing. Just unexpected—and extremely alarming.

One week later, the act of flying for Will was no longer unexpected; it was a daily experience. Nor did he any longer find it particularly alarming. Their progress through these early stages was so rapid and concentrated that none of the pupils had a moment to look back and wonder at how much they had learned. Will found that his mind was numbed by flying. They lived within sight and sound of their machines all day. They awoke to the roar of engines being run up in the hangars. They talked flying at breakfast and all other meals. From nine in the morning until six in the evening, they were either attending lectures, waiting to fly, or flying. A few more weeks of this, as one of the cadets in Will's hut remarked, and they would all turn into planes. A new cadets' class structure was created almost overnight, and its scale developed daily. At first, the elite were those who had completed a perfectly banked turn without side-slip. Later the real aristocrats did a dead-engine landing without writing off their undercarriage. Then came the biggest class division of all, between those who had soloed and those who had not. On the fifth day of flying, two cadets in the course were seen to sail triumphantly into the sky alone in their Rumptys. That evening, they basked in heroic glory, surrounded by questioners.

The first to solo was a tall dark man called Selwood. Will listened to him in the bar two evenings later. He had thick black eyebrows and a low hairline with the hair swept back and parted in the middle, and he talked in a drawling voice. "Reaction time counts for a lot, you know. People with quick reactions can compensate more rapidly, so that if a gust hits you just as you're sitting her down . . ." Selwood was already behaving like a veteran.

Will had been listening sharply because, the next morning, he was due to solo. It was a cool, dull mid-April day. The wind sock above the big hangar was barely stirring. Lieutenant Nicholls was as gray and unsmiling as the sky, and the Rumpty was drawn out of its hangar by four airmen with unemotional efficiency. Will was the first in his group of four to solo, and he already felt in a different world from them. Jones, who fancied that he should have been first, was silent; the others encouraged him with a few time-honored clichés like "Made your will, Will?"

The day's flying was in full swing. Will saw Selwood taxiing by—confident Selwood, Selwood who would soon be an ace. Even in regulation leather helmet, goggles, and fur-collared leather flying coat, and perched high up in the nacelle of a Rumpty, he had a special air about him. Two other machines took off, both cadets doing dual. Then it was Selwood's turn. His engine did not sound so crisp as the others', but he was off the ground after a short run. He was at about two hundred feet and just beyond the boundary fence when his engine began to flutter. Will did not hear it cut out, because the engine of his own Rumpty was opened out a few yards away. But Selwood's engine was dead, all right. You could even see the propeller turning over slowly in the wind. Selwood did the right thing at first and put his nose down sharply to gain speed. Then he did the wrong, but instinctive, thing. He began to turn in the hope of getting back into the field.

Will heard Nicholls shouting above the sound of the Rumpty's engine, "Don't do that, you bloody fool!" Will could see Selwood's machine momentarily poised like a kite. It stalled halfway through the turn it should never have made, its nose dropped suddenly, and it fell into a spin. It crashed into the ground just inside the fence and was splintered to pieces.

The ambulance was already on its way, bumping rapidly across the grass. "They're wasting their time," Nicholls said sharply. He turned to his four pupils. "But you haven't. That's the best lesson you could have learned before going solo. I've told you till I'm bloody blue in the face not to do that. Now you can see for yourself. If your engine cuts at takeoff, just keep going straight on, even if you have to land on a church spire. You may be near a graveyard, but you're not so likely to need it." He signaled to the fitter to cut the Rumpty's engine. "Now we'll have to wait while they clear up the mess."

The pause was a brief one. Flying weather was too valuable to waste, and it was a principle of training policy for as little notice as possible to be given to accidents. Within ten minutes, Nicholls was ordering Will into the cockpit. "Give me one circuit, then I'll get out."

The manner of Selwood's sudden death was still frozen in Will's mind as he climbed up into the cockpit; most of all, its implacable brutality. Since he had first confronted the Rumpty only a week earlier, he had seen it treated with awe by his fellow pupils and as a joke by their instructors. In fact the Rumpty was a dangerous killer. Or was it? Every airplane could be a killer if it was not handled properly, and it could kill a promising pupil as quickly as any ham-fisted fool. For the moment, he must treat it cautiously, and as a potential enemy.

"Get on with your cockpit drill," Nicholls' voice bellowed out. "Check your ailerons, check your rudder . . ."

The memory of Selwood's plunge was driven away from Will's mind by the need—the critical life-or-death need—

to concentrate on the routine of taking off in an airplane. He flew over the wreck of Selwood's machine, but the smudge of wood and canvas and dark stains of oil and petrol on the grass made no impression on his mind. "Level off at four hundred feet, then do a 180-degree banked turn to port . . ." Nicholls had told him before takeoff. For the present, the need to satisfy this hard, cynical, unsmiling instructor was the most important thing in his life.

"You'll do. Don't smash the thing." Nicholls had unstrapped himself and was climbing out before they had come to a halt on the field. Will watched him make his way back to the office block, his shoulders hunched, his body rocking in unison with his limp.

The spirit of Will Thompson left the cockpit, too, leaving only an automaton at the controls. He pushed the throttle lever wide open, and the Rumpty obediently gathered speed. The propeller torque began to pull him to one side, and he applied opposite rudder to compensate, keeping his eyes on a distant elm tree as a guide. The grass swept under him in a green blur and then fell away below. He was in the air. Stick forward a shade to keep up speed. Mustn't climb too steeply. Airspeed needle showing fifty miles an hour. All right. Back gently on the stick. Hold it like that. Altimeter needle showing one hundred feet, creeping toward the two hundred mark. Horizon down to the left. Ease back engine revolutions at four hundred feet. Keep going straight on until the railway—a dark, precisely ruled line cut diagonally through the fields—is immediately below. Then the turn. Carefully coordinated rudder and aileron.

Will went through the 180-degree turn faultlessly and was on the downwind leg of his circuit before he ceased, with awful suddenness, being an automaton and became the old familiar Will Thompson again. For five minutes, he had nothing to do but sit and steer and, in this still weather, that required no more concentration than riding a bicycle. For five minutes, Will was engulfed with a sense of appalling loneliness. He was four hundred feet up in the air, poised miraculously in an assembly of wood, wire, and canvas. Inevitably, within the next few minutes, he must return to the ground this machine in which he sat. He knew he ought to know how to do it, for he had been taught many times, and Nicholls had told him that he had not touched the controls during the last three landings they had made together.

But now, at this moment, at this height, in this airplane, he was alone. The seat behind him was empty, and there was no hand to correct his mistakes. The realization was accompanied by the first feeling of panic. It was impossible, but he had to do it.

The airfield was on his left. He could identify every familiar feature, the cluster of figures outside the office, among them the tough, brooding figure of Lieutenant Nicholls, expecting the best from him.

He was past the point where he should have cut back the throttle. With this sudden realization, Will again became part of his machine, and anxious speculation ceased. He put down the Rumpty's nose so that his body strained against the belt. The engine was just ticking over, and he could hear the wind singing in the wires and see the ground coming up sharply toward him. Level off at two hundred feet. Open throttle. 180-degree banked turn. And there, miraculously dead ahead, was the field again. He was too high. Throttle right back, steepen the dive. He wouldn't get in. He would overshoot. No, he wouldn't. It was all right. On the final approach, you always felt as if you were too high. Trust your instruments . . .

It was not a bad landing, as first solo landings go, and he was to do many worse when he was more experienced. The first bounce was no more than three or four feet, and he played the rudder pedals cleverly enough to avoid a ground loop—the ultimate humiliation. But when he taxied toward the hangars, his body was running with sweat, and he longed to tear off his helmet.

He resisted the temptation. One more task lay ahead of him. He must show no excitement. After all, a first solo was a daily event, and he must play his part properly.

Will's knees gave under him when he jumped down from the cockpit, and they continued to shake shamefully as he walked over to the group sitting or standing around the offices. Nicholls came forward to greet him, and to his astonishment his instructor's ravaged face was folding into a smile. "That wasn't bad, not bad at all," he said in his grating, cheerless voice.

They were the best words Will had ever heard. He would love this man until his dying day.

April 1917 was a bad month for the Allies. The Germans were putting up a fierce resistance on the western front. At sea, their U-boats were sinking merchantmen at a rate that must soon mean starvation for Britain. The war was not going well, and Will and his fellow pupils were badly needed. This he knew from what he heard of the air fighting: from pilots flying from France who landed at their airfield or from letters received by the instructors direct from the front. The only good news was that America had declared war on Germany, giving France and Britain a formidable new ally. But it would be many months before she had trained her new armies and shipped them to Europe. Meanwhile the Allies must fight on alone.

The mess bar in the evenings was the best place to hear the authentic, up-to-date news of squadron life. There were always one or two people in there having drinks who really knew what was going on. It was clear that April was proving to be a very bad month for the R.F.C., too. Casualties were mounting alarmingly every day. Only when the weather was dud was the R.F.C. safe. The new Albatros and Halberstadt scouts were faster, more heavily armed, better climbers, and altogether more formidable than anything the Allies had at the front. Great things were expected of new French and British scouts, and the first R.F.C. squadrons were reequipping with the marvelous S.E.5, which went into action that month. But, for the time being, the skies belonged to the German air crews, and especially the scout pilots led by great aces like Manfred von Richthofen, Rudolph Berthold, and Josef Jacobs.

Will was impatient to complete his training and to get across the Channel to the real battle. This war in the air—with its special language and terminology, its special flavors and dangers, recounted by veterans who had flown many times against the enemy—only increased his restlessness. He already felt that he was a pilot, that he had mastered the airplane. He could learn about tactics and shooting when he arrived at his squadron. He wanted to be off. His self-confidence increased when Nicholls said to him after an hour's advanced dual flying, "I'm getting rid of you tomorrow. You're going to Higher."

A few particularly promising pilots had already been picked out for an early posting to the Higher Training Squadron. The normal period at Elementary was a month, but the need for trained pilots was so acute that anyone who had reached the required standards in a shorter time could now be posted earlier.

Will had usually pleased Nicholls since his first solo flight and on one evening had been honored with an invitation to go out drinking with him. It was a mixed event. It had started off anxiously with his instructor making Will drink beer at a rate he could not comfortably match. After three almost silent pints in the empty public bar of a small inn, Nicholls cheered up, switched to whisky, and became talkative. Air fighting was all he lived for and all he would talk about—and all that Will wanted to hear. Will encouraged him, and was allowed to buy the next round. Nicholls began to emphasize his points by drawing in chalk on the darts scoreboard slate: "The way to get a Fokker's like this—see?" and he drew two curving lines across the board, intersecting as the circle narrowed. Will left the bar to take a closer look, and the floor felt like the deck of a trawler in a North Sea gale.

It was a strenuous evening, and Will became very drunk for the first time in his life. He had to be half carried home by Nicholls and was very sick in the night and felt like death the next morning. But, by lunchtime, he decided it had been worth it, especially as he could still remember a lot of the things Nicholls had told him.

All that had happened a week ago. And now Nicholls—smelly, uncouth, rude, battling, tough old Lieutenant Henry Nicholls—was getting rid of his star pupil. Will was sorry to leave him and tried to say so and to thank his instructor when he left. "Don't you get cocky" was the answer. "You're the type who does, and kills himself before he gets to a squadron. If you do make it, maybe I'll see you over Arras on a morning full of Huns. Good luck."

The next weeks formed themselves in Will's mind into a varied and rapidly changing pattern of visual images and experiences that he was too busy to consider at the time but later became a scrapbook of memories. The first page was clear and unforgettable. It was of his arrival at the new training squadron on a beautiful early May morning with the fields of Kent richly colored by fruit blossoms. A bus took him as far as the entrance to his new airfield, which nestled in a fold of the Downs. When Will got out with his duffel bag, he saw that the blue sky was full of busy airplanes, climbing and diving, turning and gliding. And these were not comic kites like the Rumpty. They were real airplanes, Avro 504s, tractor biplanes that could do sixty miles an hour. You could do anything with an Avro. And the noise of their rotary engines sounded better to Will's ears than the music of the spring birds they were drowning out.

There was an air of professionalism at this station that had been lacking at the old airfield, where a cadet might not have soloed and might not ever make a pilot.

Everywhere in the mess at lunchtime, there were new faces, and only a few he recognized. Among these was Haddow, who had arrived a week earlier after passing out from another Elementary Training Squadron. They were delighted to see each other, and Haddow was able to give him a lot of tips about life on this airfield, about the senior officers, the best flights to get into, the best hut to sleep in, about the training, and above all about the Avro—"a marvelous bus, she flies herself."

Haddow's features, voice, mannerisms, and wise, dry philosophy were to make an imperishable mark on Will's memory. They spent many evenings together, playing chess, drinking and talking in the bar or going out for walks in the long, early summer evenings, visiting villages, pubs, and churches.

After Haddow, it was the machine he flew that occupied an important place in Will's scrapbook of memories: the moment of ecstasy at first takeoff, the feeling of power and responsiveness by contrast with the Rumpty, the knowledge that you could do anything with the machine and she would enjoy it as much as you did. Even the first stall had not been especially alarming, partly because Haddow had warned him of the test the instructors put every student through without warning. At three thousand feet, in bumpy air on his second flight, Will's instructor cut the engine and pulled back the stick so that they seemed to be sinking helplessly in space. "In a few moments, I want you to take over the controls, Thompson," his instructor said in a conversational tone. "The stick will feel loose and soggy. All you have to do . . ." They might have been chatting in the mess. The engine was silent, and the only sound was the distant hum of other airplanes in the sky around them. They continued to sink toward the earth.

This was the moment when an unconfident and nervous student showed his fear and became speechless. Will was ready for it and turned around in his cockpit and responded as casually and intelligently as he could. They were at little more than fifteen hundred feet when his instructor said, "All right, now get us out of this stall." Will rapidly pushed the stick right forward, opened the Avro's throttle wide, and pumped up the fuel pressure. Within a few seconds, they were in a power dive, and he was able to pull back the stick and bring the airplane out straight and level while they were still above five hundred feet.

The first spin was a different matter and numbered among the really unpleasant experiences at higher training. This time his instructor warned him before takeoff. He was a mellow, red-faced regular army captain who had seen service in Mesopotamia and was apparently content to be an instructor until the end of the war. He said, "Today, Thompson, we will spin, and you will be alarmed. But try to watch how I get out of it." At five thousand feet they stalled, and again there was that discomforting silence. Suddenly Will's instructor kicked the left rudder, and at once the world went mad. First the horizon flicked around and around, and then it was the landscape below that spun in sickening rotation as it came up to meet them in a riot of green and pink and white. Will clutched tightly at the cockpit ledge. He was strapped in, but his belt was digging deeply into his stomach and he felt as if a new, unknown power was attempting to cast him into space. Then, as quickly, the rotation ceased, and they were going straight down, the green becoming clear geometric fields, the pink and white the safe, familiar orchards of Kent.

But, within a week, Will had done his first solo spin and had looped-the-loop, hanging upside down for too long the first time so that he had nearly spun out. The next time, it was better. The third time, he pulled himself out on top to perform a fair Immelmann. And then he felt that he had tamed the Avro, that it was as docile and obedient to his commands as the border collie bringing down the sheep from the fells above Amplethwaite.

New pleasures came with his renewed self-confidence. Late one evening, he played among the clouds, swooping around and over them in the last of the sunlight. Below him, the world had turned dark gray. It was already dusk down there. Will put the Avro's nose down in a power dive. The engine screamed, and for the first time he saw one hundred miles an hour on the airspeed indicator. At two hundred feet, the sun had set, and a distant steam locomotive cut a red glow across the Weald of Kent. Will knew he should land. His was the last plane in the sky. But he was consumed with a new ecstasy, as if he must fly forever and could fly forever with this wonderful machine in his hands. So he climbed again at full throttle, and slowly, as if he could control even the world's timeless rotation, a new dawn began to break, and the sun rose slowly again above the horizon and filled his cockpit with its scarlet light.

That night Haddow and he walked eight miles in the moonlight, became lost, and had to crawl back under the airfield's perimeter wire at one o'clock.

The art and technique of flying fascinated Haddow as much as Will, and they both delighted equally in the beauty it revealed to the senses. "By God, I wish I could paint," Haddow said one day. "What couldn't an impressionist do with the Folkestone cliffs at dawn seen through scattered cumulus!" Will had been up on the first flight that morning, too. "After the war, we ought to buy up cheap one of those big jobs, those new Handley Page bombers, and hire it out to artists. Five pounds an hour, pilot included. We'd make a fortune."

Will, too, could not imagine life without flying. But he could not imagine life without war, either, and daily the final purpose of their training became increasingly evident. Already they had learned how to strip and assemble a Lewis gun and a Vickers machine gun. Twice a week, they went to the target or clay pigeon range to practice shooting, and toward the end of their course, they went in groups to another airfield where for the first time they learned how to handle a gun in the air, how to allow for deflection, and how to comprehend the secrets of the new Aldis sight. The imminence of the business of killing came home to Will on the morning when he pulled the Lewis trigger and watched the tracer bullets spitting from the muzzle and streaming in deadly procession toward the ground target. The acrid smell, the ugly sound, the metallic vibration in his hand were all a part of the reality of the war in which he was soon to fight.

The idea of formation flying fascinated Will, and he was impatient to try it. They had been told that it was a treacherous business at first, that it was a skill to be learned only when you were fully proficient. But Will knew that he was ready for it. He discussed the matter with Haddow, and they agreed that it would be highly satisfying to impress their instructors with their skill when they later had their first lesson.

The following morning they arranged to fly at the same time and to rendezvous over a railway station at five thousand feet and a safe twenty miles away. Will was first off and climbed up to over six thousand feet, the highest he had ever been, and waited up sun for Haddow to appear. He saw the biplane laboring along against the gusty west wind, and when it was just below him, he turned over on his back and made a simulated attack from behind as if Haddow were a German two-seater pilot on patrol.

Will achieved complete surprise and closed right in to thirty yards, imagining that he was filling the machine with bullet holes. At the last second, he pushed forward the stick, went under the Avro, and pulled up alongside. Haddow realized that he had been surprised. Will saw him hold up his arms in mock surrender and mouth the word "*Kamerad!*" They pushed up their goggles and laughed.

Will found formation flying surprisingly difficult. Haddow was the leader, and Will brought his Avro in, attempting to tuck his wings behind Haddow's. But however delicately he handled his controls and however hard he tried to anticipate the movement of the other machine, he found himself rising and falling too abruptly to risk tucking his wings behind the other pair. At twenty feet distance, he could match the speed and the vertical movements reasonably accurately, but every time he attempted to close in, it seemed they must collide.

In the end, he had to admit defeat. Haddow raised his right hand and waved him into the lead, and then attempted to formate on Will's Avro. He was no more successful. Will thought the bumpy weather might be to blame. All the same, it was irritating. They had often seen the instructors doing it, five in V formation, wings almost brushing one another, in perfect configuration. Will concentrated on flying as steadily as he could, and Haddow came in closer than before. This was not at all bad. Haddow's wing tips were just behind his own, and for several seconds they held together steadily. A small air pocket upset the pattern, and Will dropped more sharply than Haddow. They had almost regained their former position when they hit a bigger pocket, and Haddow's upper wing tip touched Will's lower wing.

The effect was fearful and instantaneous. The two machines shot apart as if suddenly stung. The wing tip of Will's Avro had been crumpled. He felt oddly unbalanced, and he sat numbed by a terrible fear, waiting for the wing to fall apart. Nothing worse happened, and he found he could hold course and height by keeping the stick well over. Then he looked for Haddow.

When he saw his friend out of control below, and falling fast, he was filled with a new and different agony of fear and began to shout appeals to save him. "Oh no, no, no—you can't, you can't!" he cried. He pushed forward his stick and tried to catch up with him in a dive, with the wild idea of coming alongside and plucking him out. The crippled Avro was falling fast in a series of spiraling swoops, each of which was followed by a stall. He could see that half the wing was missing and that the outer struts were trailing like a flight commander's streamers. At any moment, the frail structure seemed as if it must fall apart.

Will never caught up. He got close enough to see the dark figure of Haddow in the cockpit, and he imagined him struggling to regain balance and control of his crippled machine. He seemed to be aiming for a copse, with the idea that it might be safer to crash into trees, but he failed, and at about a hundred feet, the fluttering wreck went into a stall and then a spin. Will wanted to look away and could not. From five hundred feet above, he watched in paralyzed horror the dying throes of the Avro as it turned and turned and, even before Will expected it to happen, flattened itself out in the corner of a small field, the pieces spreading wide like a plate dropped on a stone floor.

Will knew that he could have made a successful crash landing beside the wreck and was tempted to do so. But there were already farm laborers from the next field running toward it. He could do nothing to help and might add to their troubles by injuring himself. His duty was clear: He must return to his base and direct an ambulance to the spot as soon as he could.

But then what could an ambulance do? One in ten was the accepted rate of survival from spinning in. Haddow must be dead. Will had killed him. It was his idea to try formation flying. Too young, too inexperienced, too self-confident—just as Nicholls had warned him. He would be court-martialed. They would find out his age; he would be sent back to school. But what did all that matter? The sharp, intelligent, cynical mind was stilled, and that stocky figure would never pace beside him again over the fields of Kent.

With the wind behind him, Will was back over his airfield in fifteen minutes and made a bad landing, coming in too fast in case his stalling speed had been affected by the loss of his wing tip. When he taxied in toward the hangars, he saw people converging on him. They might merely have been curious about his damaged wing, but in his guilt-ridden and grief-stricken condition, Will saw them as a hostile lynch mob, ready to exact revenge for the death of Haddow.

"You had better take up A2636 and do some circuits and bumps." To his astonishment, Will had been sent down to the hangars again after recounting briefly to his instructor what had happened. There had been no arrest, no rebuke even. He had just been ordered up into the air, quickly, before his nerve broke. No one else spoke to him; only the fitter standing with his hands on the propeller: "Ignition on? Contact, sir." The rotary burst into life, chocks were cleared, and Will taxied out. It was nine thirty; breakfast was still being served in the officers' mess. How could so many momentous and awful things have happened in such a short part of a day?

He flew for fifteen minutes with his mind dazed and did three landings, each by instinct rather than by conscious calculation. Then he was ordered to report to the commanding officer. The wind had brought up squalls, and the rain was pouring so hard down the office windows that the airfield was obscured, symbolically shutting him off from the world of flying. Major Hawker was at his desk, his service-soiled hat beside a pile of papers. Will had listened to him lecture, crisply and in a hoarse voice. He was a lean, short man with the Military Cross ribbon below his wings, and had flown Blériots as long ago as 1914. Will saluted and stood to attention.

"Your friend is not dead, you'll be surprised to hear." Will reached forward and clutched at the edge of the desk. "All right, sit down in that chair."

Will continued to stare in disbelief at the major from his new lower level and heard him say above the sound of the beating rain, "He won't fly for a while, but he will live, so the M.O. informs me. He was very lucky. A suspected fractured skull, a broken leg, and a lot of cuts. What happened?"

Will was determined to tell the truth. "I first saw him over Nethermere station, sir, below me, so I did a mock attack from astern, closed in, and then—"

"Oh, so that was it," broke in the major. "I applaud your keenness, and I've got these good reports on your progress. But you don't want to get ahead of yourself. There'll be plenty of opportunity for mock dogfighting and real dogfighting later. So you clipped his wing. Easy enough thing to do. But bloody careless. There'll be a Court of Inquiry, of course, and you'll give your evidence in detail then. You're dismissed."

So Will found himself in a false and uncomfortable position. He had left the C.O. with the impression that the collision had been caused by an excess of fighting zeal rather than an idiotic attempt at formation flying. Later in the day, he thought of writing an official note to him but decided to tell Haddow's parents exactly what had happened. Everything would come out in the Court of Inquiry.

Crashes were too common at this, the most dangerous period of training, for Will's to be discussed for long. There were two more in the same week, one killing an instructor and pupil at takeoff. Here in summer, deep in the peaceful heart of the Kent countryside, they were being hardened to the wastage of war and learning with their flying skill to shrug off the loss of friends and accept the gaps at the mess table. Will became friends with a boy called Henderson who was only eighteen and was as keen on speed and his motor bicycle as the vicar at Amplethwaite. They roared along the Kent lanes at dusk, and it was nearly as good as flying. But they did not stop at the churches, and Will sorely missed Haddow's keen mind and dry wit. He was not allowed even a day's leave to visit him. He knew that an apology would only enrage Haddow, so he wrote about flying and the other pupil pilots and reminisced about their days together.

At the end of June, Will was taken up for a final wings check by the major. The Court of Inquiry had taken place the week before, and the major, who had presided, showed that he thought Will had deliberately deceived him. There was an official reprimand, and a note was made in his log-book. Dictated evidence from Haddow in hospital stated only that he could remember nothing after takeoff. Will was to reflect on this ruefully, as he could as well have stuck to his original unwittingly abbreviated account.

The major made it clear that he did not care for Will by putting the Avro through a series of hair-raising maneuvers for nearly an hour and then spinning from six thousand feet, ending up by flying low for miles along the cliff tops, touching the Avro's wheels several times. He appeared satisfied only when Will leaned out and was sick. Then the major gave the signal for him to take over the controls, and the test began. The major's cruel petulance had an effect on Will that was quite different from what the major had intended. Will was so angry that he flew better than he had ever flown before, and in the final test—a dead-engine landing into a fifty-yard circle—he touched down to a perfect three-pointer plumb in the center.

The major walked away without a word. But Will's name was up on the bulletin board the next day. He had ranked third, and on July 1 he was sent off on three days' leave with a pair of wings sewn to his jacket. The bright gold on his left breast kept catching his eye, and when he was certain no one was looking, he could not resist glancing down at the crown and wings of the fully fledged aviator spreading out from the proud initials R.F.C. Now he was prepared to go home on leave and risk facing Vicky.

Will thought carefully about how he would find Amplethwaite and all his friends after this long separation. But his first anxiety was for how he would react to their new view of him, the reserved and quiet boy who had lost his girl and surprised them all by going off to the war. He knew that he had done nothing yet, except to make a decision and act on it and acquire a new skill. He was no hero, but he knew that some people would regard him as one, and he dreaded, above all, being seen under false colors. He felt that in many ways he had grown six years in little more than six months. And yet, he thought, if only he could manage his relations with all those most dear to him as well as he could roll an Avro, he would feel happier about his leave!

He had few worries about his parents. He had written to them regularly, and he knew that his mother now completely understood why he had left. He longed to see them both again, to feel the familiar furniture of his home under his hands and the floors beneath his feet. He longed, too, after months of deprivation of rocks and mountains, for the sight of the running becks and the new year's bracken, and above all for the fells. It was about his friends that he felt disquiet. How would they be, how would he be, when they met? He must avoid being patronizing. That was the greatest danger, for he was fully conscious of the need to avoid a swagger in his walk: The mere hint of self-conceit made the blood rush to his cheeks.

And then, of course, there was Vicky. For every week he had been away, he had grown another thin layer of protective skin over the wound. And yet still the scar throbbed at night sometimes, and he felt a deep protective tenderness toward the remote and pretty schoolgirl she had become in his mind. The memory of the shame she had caused him still stung, but he also knew that today he would never have allowed such grief to overwhelm him. His horizon, in fact, had broadened in the same way that it spread out from a climbing plane; but there, standing on it whenever he had time to remember her, was the neat, stalwart, darling figure of Vicky—little Vicky as he now thought of her, the girl who had forced him out to face the real world.

When he first arrived, it seemed that nothing had changed and that only he was different. The choir was at practice when he walked up from the bus stop past the school, and the thought that his own voice might have been one of the tenor chorus—with Tom Filton, Jim Shore, Albert Storey, and the others—made him realize how suddenly the gap had grown. Old Mother Bell was at the post office counter, mixing her bacon with the stamps as always, and she waved in her old way at Will as he passed, too nearsighted to recognize his uniform and too slow in her mind now to realize she had not seen him for months.

The homecoming was perfect. Will knew that it would be from the moment he saw his mother running out of the kitchen to kiss him. She left flour on his wings when she brushed them admiringly with her fingertips, and they laughed. They laughed all through supper, and his father watched them approvingly and asked man-to-man questions about how an airplane worked. Then Will walked up high on the fells until midnight, when there was still a faint glow above the Irish Sea, and slept at last to the sound of beck water instead of running airplane engines.

He met his friends in his old civilian clothes, and that made everything easier. To his surprise, Will found that they had changed a great deal, too, and they obviously felt as grown-up and responsible as he did. There was no horseplay, only a little lighthearted banter at first. Then they were very serious and earnest together as they leaned over the bridge parapet and watched the water slip by and discussed their futures. Within six months they would all be fighting, and the chances that they would all survive were very slim. They agreed to meet again at this same place at twelve noon on the twelfth day of the twelfth month of 1918, whether or not the war was over by then.

The vicar had gone off to France as a chaplain soon after Will had left the village. "One Sunday after evensong, he just got on his motor bicycle, opened the throttle wide, and went. You could hear his engine bellowing halfway to Hawkshead," Tom told Will.

He did not see Vicky, and no one mentioned her until the last day. Then Tom's Elizabeth told him that she had gone away to stay for a week in Liverpool a few days before Will was due home on leave. "I think she's gone for an interview as a nurse," Elizabeth told Will. "She'll be sorry to have missed you."

"I don't think so," Will said.

"Oh, but you're wrong. She's so proud of you. She wants to see you in your uniform."

Will half believed what he heard and felt himself torn by a number of contradictory emotions and memories: of how he desperately wanted to catch the scent of her hair, how savagely cruel she had been, how she had thrown their love away because of a stumble. "She's so proud of you!" What business had she to be proud of him—as if she personally had made a pilot of him? But her standards were the highest —she liked only winners, no second best for Vicky.

He wished her name had not been mentioned.

But a most curious thing happened that was even more disturbing. Will took the train back to London on a Monday morning. He remembered the last time he had made this journey and how innocent and yet determined he had been.

This time he was overwhelmed by a feeling of melancholy, for he knew how unlikely it was that he would ever again see the blue gray silhouette of the Lakeland fells; and he considered how this train journey was now marking a third decisive phase in his recent life.

The train halted briefly at Staveley, and while several passengers got in or out, the train from the south drew in to the opposite platform. Will noticed that there were four people in the compartment a few feet away, and he did not recognize any of them. His train began to move slowly forward, and the next window came into view. Vicky was already struggling to open the window as Will stood up and grasped the leather strap to pull down his own. There were perhaps three seconds when both windows were open and Will and Vicky could look unbelievingly at each other across the gap, and there was time for only one of them to speak. Vicky uttered only two words as they were drawn relentlessly apart amid the sound of turning wheels and escaping steam. "Oh, Will!" she called. It was a heartrending appeal, unmistakably and at once a cry of remorse and love and despair. The sound of her voice and the memory of her distraught face haunted him all the way to London.

Will heard the guns for the first time when the troopship docked at Calais, France. It might have been thunder, and the impression that this was only a summer storm was heightened by the mountainous black clouds that dominated the eastern sky. The young infantry officer leaning on the rail beside him said wearily, "There's a big push on. I'll bet the rain's coming down in buckets. It always does. And, God, the mud! My company will be sunk without trace by the time I get to them."

Halted on a railway track three hours later, Will put his head out of the compartment window. He could feel the vibration through the sill on which he rested his hands and the floorboards beneath his feet. The gunfire sounded like the nearby beat of a hundred bass drums. It was eleven o'clock at night, but the reflected glow of the gunflashes bathed the fields and hedges and trees in a ghostly yellow light. A tall cavalry officer, who was sitting beside Will and had read Ovid in silence from Calais, remarked that it was all very Wagnerian and tedious, and advised Will to sleep while he could.

It was good advice, for as the night advanced and the train crept by slow stages nearer to the front, the intensity of light and sound increased until, by dawn, sleep was possible only to old campaigners. At seven o'clock, the train halted for the last time, and for the very good reason that there was no more line—as Will saw when he stepped down onto the temporary wooden platform. Twice, he was told, the war had passed over this railway, and he could see ahead the scattered shell holes, some raw and new, and others already half-healed by summer flowers and sprouting grass.

A shattered farmhouse was the assembly point. Drawn up beside it were a dozen open trucks and a pair of ambulances from which wounded men on stretchers were being removed and carried toward the train. Up a muddy lane that rose toward the crest of a hill marched a platoon of infantry in tin helmets and carrying rifles, shoulders hunched against the light drizzle. They were passing the remains of a truck that had received a direct shell hit, its hood pointing in hopeless disarray to the sky. Two fields away to the north, a battery of heavy artillery—the figures of the busy gunners and their weapons just visible beneath their camouflage netting—was firing at regular intervals. At every discharge, the dark sky was slashed yellow white; the crash was like a physical blow, and the air seemed to be torn apart. The scene of damage, violence, and apparent disorganization was a summation of modern war. Only the act of death was missing, and that was not far away.

"Thompson? You're on for Bildaut," said the R.T.O. He had a dead cigarette in one hand, a list in the other. So there was some organization. Will was directed to one of the trucks, which was already full of other ranks and two sergeants, many from his squadron and back from Blighty.

He was given a seat and treated respectfully. "First time out, sir?" enquired one of the sergeants. "You'll be all right with us, now that we've got Camels. We're knocking the living daylights out of them. Done many hours in them, sir?"

"Just one," Will admitted. "No time for more."

The last weeks had been a hustle, with gunnery and bombing practice on any machine he could find at the post-graduation course. Every Camel, like every pilot, was badly needed at the front. There had been only one machine at the airfield, and that had been crashed by the next pilot to fly it. For the Camel was a tricky bus—marvelous but tricky. The Pup had already been outclassed by this new Sopwith plane, which could fly faster and was even more maneuverable. The Camel had twice the firepower of the Pup, with two Vickers machine guns firing through the arc of the propeller. In skilled hands, it was the master of any German plane in the sky. "Kick, right rudder," he had been told at the postgraduation course, "and you're going back the way you were coming before you can say 'Richthofen.' "

And now Will was to fly the Camel in war. All that he had been working toward was about to take place. He was joining a crack scout squadron on the western front as a fully qualified pilot. And his time of arrival had coincided with one of the greatest pushes of the war.

An orderly carried Will's bags from the guard room along the duck-boarded track, past an antiaircraft gun pit and several slit trenches, to the officers' mess, a long camouflaged tent on the edge of the field. A flight of six Camels had just broken through the clouds and was circling before coming in. Will told the orderly to put his bags on his bed and watched the machines come in. They touched down quickly in turn with the professional nonchalance of long practice, and taxied in toward the line of canvas hangars.

How excitingly ferocious they looked! They were a shade larger than the Pup, and the lower wing had a marked dihedral. The other feature that made them so immediately identifiable was the prominent cover to the breeches of the twin Vickers guns set in front of the cockpit, the "hump" that gave the machine its name. The Camel was a real killer, the most feared fighting plane on the western front.

The flight commander's machine trailing his streamers was the first to come to a halt, and Will watched the captain pull off his helmet and leap nimbly to the ground. A table had been set up on the grass outside a tent, and the pilots in their fur-collared leather jackets gathered around it to report to the intelligence officer. Will joined the outside of the circle, unnoticed by the others.

The flight commander was talking in short staccato sentences. He was a chubby-faced boy with a snub nose covered in freckles. He looked sixteen and could not have been more than nineteen. Will noticed that his nicotine-stained finger on the map was shaking, and as he talked he kept blowing away the spilled cigarette ash. "Christ, what a way to run a war!" he was saying in a high-pitched voice. "We were scraping the ground to keep out of the cloud. What's the use of sending us up in weather like this? Sheer bloody murder. Bob, you saw them," he said to one of his pilots, "over the line they were even using pistols and you could see which Huns had gold fillings. We picked up about a hundred machine-gun bullets, and God only knows how any of us got back."

"Did you find anything?" asked the intelligence officer.

"It was a bit clearer in Hunland, and we found Holle Bosch wood, what's left of it. No sign of the Fees we were supposed to be looking after, though. Probably had more sense and stayed at home. Saw a couple of Hun two-seaters, probably Rumplers. But they blew off east as soon as they spotted us. I'll bet every other Hun was on the ground, wise birds. It wasn't fit for sparrows. Even Archie couldn't believe his eyes and forgot to fire at us."

The flight commander stood up and pulled off his flying coat. "You'd better get some breakfast," he told his pilots. "The bar open yet, Spy?" he asked the intelligence officer. "I need a warmer." He saw Will for the first time and briefly looked him up and down as if to assess his potential for the first team. Then he stepped forward and gripped Will's hand hard and offered him a cigarette. "You're Thompson, aren't you. Good. Expecting you. Have a good trip up? Flown Camels much? They're very splitarse, you know. Like a fiery girl. Tough at first but fun to play with when you get used to them. Come on, have a drink. You're in my flight—B. Very good flight, too. Only lost one pilot last week, and he was a fool."

The commander's name was Johnny Watson. He had been out six months and was beginning to show it. He had a score of nine, had been shot down twice, and had somehow survived the April German scourge. Will noticed that he used two hands to hold his glass of whisky and that the clear blue eyes, by contrast with the chubby innocence of his face, had the glint of the fanatic.

They had two large drinks while Watson told him what they were doing—escorting bombers and photographic reconnaissance machines, looking for Germans, especially unescorted two-seaters, bagging balloons, machine-gunning trenches when things were sticky on the ground. "Any damn thing and they're all hell," he told Will, staring at the end of his second drink and holding his glass with fingers that were steadier now. "I'll get someone to show you your bed, then you'd better take up a kite and get the feel of the

Camel." He started to order another drink and changed his mind. "Better not get tight; there's another show at three o'clock."

Will was not used to whisky at any time, and two doubles in the middle of the morning had sent his head reeling, and he had difficulty holding a straight line out of the mess behind Watson. But his flight commander appeared quite unaffected except that he seemed more cheerful and did not use so many expletives. He called to a passing airman to show Will to his hut and made for his office.

There were three other pilots in Will's hut, all stretched out on their beds, fully clothed and asleep after their early start. Will was thankful for the chance to close his eyes after an almost sleepless night. He was awakened an hour later by their voices. Two of them were playing chess, and the third was watching. They all turned when Will sat up, and greeted him cheerfully.

"How's the midday hangover?" asked one, a tall dark Scot who introduced himself simply as Mac. "An alcoholic hour with Johnny on arrival is really diving in at the deep end. What's more, you're on the three o'clock job whether you like it or not. Someone's gone sick and we're a man short."

Will looked at the three of them in disbelief. He was still heavy with sleep and had not yet accustomed himself to his new surroundings. A show? Today? Before he had unpacked? They must be joking. But this was no leg-pull, as Mac explained. The pressure was on. Every machine was needed. "That's fine," Will said at last. "A bit of a surprise, that's all. Now you blokes had better tell me what it's all about."

They were a good crowd in the hut. Besides Mac, there was a lanky ginger-haired boy called Arthur Campbell, with white eyelashes, who blinked and stuttered a great deal, played a good game of chess, and (rather surprisingly because he looked slow) was very fast with the girls and a very hot pilot indeed—so Mac told him later. Then there was the fire-eater, Douglas Raven, a real German-hater, who was a devil for jobs and was obviously set for a high score and a flight of his own before his time was up. Mac told Will later that Raven had got four already and that he was a good man to fly with because he had eyes that could pick out a German two-seater at five miles and could smell Fokkers through a cloud bank.

All three were veterans by R.F.C. standards, having been with the squadron for more than three months and having survived the holocaust of April, when they were very green and the Germans very aggressive. They had all seen numbers of new pilots like Will arrive on the squadron, full of fearless eagerness, survive maybe a week or two, and then plummet down from a dogfight—sometimes in flames, never to be seen again—or go into the ground suddenly, riddled by machine-gun fire.

At one o'clock, they left the hut for lunch. "Just don't try anything fancy for a bit," Campbell advised. "We'll all be looking after you. And if it comes to a scrap, just remember you can outturn anything in a Camel."

The major saw Will briefly after lunch. He was very crisp and impersonal and hardly looked at him as he spoke. "We normally give new pilots a few days to settle in. But we're busy just now, as you can hear. You'll be all right after a couple of jobs. And by tonight, you won't be the most junior officer. We've got two more arriving." His eyes caught Will's for the first time. "You'll be like a veteran to them," he said wryly.

Like everything else at Bildaut, the briefing was casual. Johnny Watson stabbed with an angry finger at the big wall map and said in his high voice, "It's a trench strafe here," and everyone groaned. "There'll be three other flights from La Lovie on the same job, so look out for them and don't get mixed up. After that, we'll probably climb up over Hunland and see what's going on, and come back around here." His dark eyes ranged briefly over his pilots and picked out Will. "Thompson, you'll fly number two to Mac, and watch his tail."

That was all. They strolled over to the hangars, pulling on their heavy coats and gloves as if they were going out beagling on a winter's afternoon. Their six Camels were ready for them; the mechanics were standing by. The weather had cleared, and the wind had died, and the thunder of the guns to the east was louder than ever.

Mac pointed at the most distant machine. "That's yours. Just follow and stick close to me. Kick your rudder like hell if the ground fire gets hot. It puts them off their aim."

There was no time for introspection or nervousness. Things were happening so fast that Will had to give all his thoughts to each procedure, stage by stage. But subconsciously, the loyalty to these men of his flight was hardening within him, the process accelerated by their unity of purpose, by his training, and by the determination to show up favorably to his flight commander and the men whose dangerous life he had suddenly joined.

Will dropped into the snug seat of the Camel's cockpit. "Nice to have you with us, sir," said the mechanic who helped to buckle his belt. It was the most formal greeting he had heard since he had arrived eight hours earlier.

Will glanced quickly around the cockpit, at the three instruments showing engine speed, airspeed, and height. Those were the ignition switches on the left; he remembered that from his flight two weeks ago. The spade-handled stick between his legs felt just right, and his feet rested comfortably on the rudder bars. Dominating the cockpit were the breeches of the two Vickers machine guns, and between them the long tube of the Aldis sight. It was all very purposeful and businesslike. No wonder everyone liked the Camel, at least those who survived its temperament and enemy fire.

All the other engines were running, and the flight commander was taxiing out, and Will was still fussing with the starting procedure. He set the fuel mixture at full rich and called out "Contact!" The order was repeated by the mechanic swinging the propeller, and at once the 110-horsepower Clerget rotary burst into life.

Mac signaled to Will as he passed, waving him on. "Chocks away," Will shouted. He opened the throttle wider and hastened to catch up with the other Camel.

Will had never seen such speed. Watson was already in the air, and two more Camels were accelerating across the grass right behind him. He skipped over almost all the checks he had been carefully trained to follow at flying school, and still he was slowest off the ground. But, with the throttle wide open, he was soon in the air and remembered just in time to lean the fuel mixture; otherwise the rotary would have choked, and that could quickly lead to a spin-in. By banking steeply and cutting a corner, he came up alongside Mac, who gave him a quick wave and signaled him in closer.

At last Will could relax and look about him. Below there was a railway line, dead straight, cutting through the green landscape; a lake, a useful landmark to remember if he was ever lost: harp-shaped, the sharper end pointing toward the airfield.

The six close-bunched Camels of B Flight made a grand sight. Surely, he thought, there had never been a more beautiful instrument of war. Together they were so powerful, with their twelve machine guns and their experienced pilots, that it seemed no one would brave them. Like this, they were invulnerable.

At three thousand feet, Watson took them around a small cloud, and then they began to dive. Below, Will could see a blotchy gray green spread of landscape like a bad complexion, pockmarked haphazardly with shell holes and scored with trench lines, some straight, some curved, some zigzagging without apparent plan or purpose. They were approaching the front, which Will had imagined would be parallel lines of opposing trenches, each manned by regularly spaced infantry shooting at one another. Instead the western front, at least on this Fifth Army sector, was an untidy mess of torn fields and wrecked roads, threaded with careless lines as if by some mad seamstress and from which there was no sign of life.

At first glance, it looked as if a giant had driven a great punch into the map, and then left the lifeless pulp of ground. A more careful look showed that the perennial activity of living and killing was taking place. What remained of a village church was smoldering, puffs that suddenly sprouted from the earth and marked shell bursts, and it was just possible to make out groups of figures and horses and trucks moving mindlessly to and fro. A great battle was going on down there, intermittently and in confused disorder. And now Will Thompson was to take a small part in it.

The flight went down in a long spiral. At one point in the descent, Will found himself looking down into the flight commander's cockpit some two hundred feet below, and he could see Watson examining closely the map stretched out over his knees and then looking out to check his position against the ground below. They went over the rearmost British trenches at a hundred feet. How could anyone live down there? The earth had been battered into lifelessness, and every shell hole was a foul brown pool. Between them, there floundered groups of men in tin hats carrying rifles, and some of them looked up and waved as the Camels flew low overhead. Barbed-wire entanglements, piled-up sandbags, more shell holes, and entrenchments shot past Will's wing tips in a blur. He saw Watson bank steeply and then dive even lower. Flashes of fire shot from his machine guns. They were attacking.

The next seconds were bewildering and confusing and more frightening than Will could have believed possible. They had flashed over the lines before he had realized it, and now everything was being thrown at them: rifle fire, machine guns, and heavier stuff too. All around them, the air was being cut to pieces, and it seemed impossible that a single Camel could find space to fly in.

Will remembered Mac's advice and kicked left and right rudder in turn so that his machine slewed from side to side. At first, he was too busy keeping his Camel under control to see what they were supposed to be shooting at. Then he saw Mac dropping his nose and firing along a deep trench crammed with field gray figures, all firing back at the intruders. Will went down after him, got the trench in his sight, and gave a long burst with his guns, feeling his machine shuddering under the recoil, and smelling the rich scent of spent cordite.

Figures were tumbling beneath him. Half-sickened, half-intoxicated with the heady sense of power, Will followed the other machines in a loose line around to the left and down onto a communication trench. There were men coming up to it, bowed down under their packs, innocent half-troglodytes who were safe from shellfire but not from probing scout pilots who had the nerve to flush them out.

The Camels were so low, their wheels were almost touching the parapets, and Will found himself lifting up at the last split second to clear a stack of barbed-wire rolls. There was time for two more bursts before Watson suddenly shot up in a climbing turn, pursued by a fountain of gunfire, some of it tracer that bisected his course in long yellow lines. They followed him at full throttle, thrusting wildly up to the greater safety of three thousand feet to re-form.

The wind was cold against Will's cheeks, but he could feel the sweat trickling down his body, his feet were unsteady on the rudder pedals, and his teeth were chattering. How could they all have survived that holocaust of fire? And yet B Flight was intact, and all six machines were cruising in close formation at ninety miles an hour, heading deeper into German-held territory.

He saw Mac glance across at him. He grinned and pointed at Will's tail. Will looked back over his shoulder and saw that the rear end of his fuselage and his elevators were riddled with holes. At the same moment, a battery of heavy guns opened up on them, spotting the sky ahead and below with ugly dark blobs. *Whooomph, whooomph, whooomph!* they went, spitting out their wanton steel fragments and tossing the air about.

A shell burst close under Will's tail, and his Camel gave a lurch that almost threw it on its back. B Flight opened up and took evasive action individually, each machine dropping or rising and making sharp, flat turns to confuse the gunners five thousand feet below.

Will could see the other pilots turning their heads from side to side, searching the sky, and he followed their example. There was not much to see. Two or three miles away, some Harry Tates back from a bombing raid were attracting Archie's attention, and high above, their wing tips catching the sun, were two flights of scouts—they might have been

Pups or Camels—making their way into Germany. Toward the sun was the direction to watch, Will knew, and every few seconds he turned and held his gloved hand against it to scrutinize this dangerous blind spot.

Watson pulled his nose up, and they began to climb again at three-quarter throttle, weaving to right and left in search of prey. The Germans were curiously quiet in the air, and even Archie seemed to have tired of wasting ammunition. They were far into German-held territory and at twelve thousand feet. Will had only once before been above ten thousand, and it was bitterly cold. The land below was untouched by the savagery of war, the fields green or golden with harvest-ripe corn. Far to the south, a dark green forest stretched interminably into the distant haze, bisected by a winding river. Up here the sun was so clear, the air so clean, the landscape so serene, it suddenly seemed unbelievable to Will that half an hour earlier he had been killing men at close range and had come near to death himself.

"Never trust the bloody sky," that coarse-tongued instructor, Henry Nicholls, had once told Will. "When it's all peaceful, that's the time some sod will be under your tail at thirty yards with his finger on his Spandaus." And Will noticed how the others were constantly weaving and turning their heads. To stay alive at this game, you could not relax for a second. Watson demonstrated this a few minutes later. Will saw him waggle his wings and then peel off to the left with Campbell and Raven following, Mac keeping the other three up above. Four thousand feet below, a tiny dark square against the dark ground, Will could just make out a two-seater heading east. Johnny Watson might be drinking a great deal too much whisky, but his eyesight was still all right.

Will watched the primeval drama with a feeling of mixed horror and excitement. The three Camels, diving straight out of the sun, rapidly diminished in size until they were behind and no larger than the German two-seater. He saw Watson, well ahead of the other two, flatten out and pull up under the German, which continued on its way in seeming ignorance of its imminent end. Surely the pilot must take some evasive action! Will heard himself shout ridiculously, "Look out!" At the same moment, the two-seater twitched as if kicked hard and assumed an impossible posture in the sky. Watson had got in a single, long, and fatal burst at point-blank range.

Will could just make out that one of the two-seater's wings had folded. A flash of flame, at first like a distant spark and then an all-consuming blaze, spread over the length of the machine. For a few seconds, the airplane seemed to remain poised helplessly in the sky, and then it turned over and plummeted down, trailing a long line of smoke like a finger pointing toward its grave.

At once, as if awakened to a fury of revenge, Archie opened up, blackening the sky about the three triumphant Camels. Will saw Watson complete a disdainful loop of victory and climb back with Campbell and Raven to rejoin the rest of his flight.

Douglas Raven collapsed on his bed and reached out for his cigarettes. "Now you know how it's done," he said to Will. "Nasty sight, isn't it?" He turned to the other two, who were still taking off their flying gear. "Johnny Watson's a greedy devil. Doesn't give a fellow a chance."

"But a damn good s-s-shot, you've got to admit," Campbell said. "Anyway, it's your t-t-turn now, Doug."

"What do you mean?" Will asked.

"Our dear old flight commander is off to Blighty tomorrow, with ten confirmed victories and an M.C. There's going to be an almighty binge tonight to celebrate the occasion. And Doug is taking over the flight, the good Lord help us all."

They all lay on their beds, and Will savored the peace and contentment, the satisfaction of having survived his first job, and the pleasure of being accepted on equal terms both in the flight and in this shared hut. There was a tremendous amount still to learn, and his mind was full of questions, but he recognized that these minutes before dinner seemed to be reserved for quiet contemplation or conversation. He must not seem too eager.

The renewal of the fear that had struck like a lance blow at the bottom of his stomach when they were trench-strafing hit Will again at the end of the party. Perhaps it was the weakening effect of all the alcohol. But the common theory was that whisky was an insulator against fear; that's why nearly everyone drank it in such quantities. Or it may have been the realization of the inevitability of the next day, which was now only a few hours away. A Flight was doing the early morning show, and its pilots had gone off to bed dutifully early and more or less sober. At about one o'clock, Arthur Campbell paced uncertainly on his long legs across the mess bar to Will, with a full glass of whisky in one hand, and poked Will in the ribs with the other hand. His stutter was more pronounced after an evening of drinking, and he had difficulty in delivering his statement.

"Evening sh-sh-show for us, ol' boy. Plenty of t-t-time, so drink up." Before Will could answer, there was an outbreak of lighthearted fighting in which two chairs were smashed, and Johnny Watson was stood on the bar and ordered to make a speech. He did so, with spirit, told them

B Flight was the best flight in the squadron, which was the best squadron in the R.F.C., and that his M.C. belonged to them all really. "I've just got to wear the bloody thing, and the only advantage of that," he concluded, raising his glass for another toast, "is that I'll get more girls panting after me than the rest of you put together." This was received with a loud chorus of boos, and the barmen were set to work again.

At two o'clock, Mac rescued Will, who was feeling sick and tired. Will was relieved to see that he had drunk very little. "You had better come to bed, you must be whacked," Mac said. There was something reassuring about his heavy Scots accent, too.

It was a clear starlit night outside, and as they walked across to the hut, the sound of the guns began to match and then overwhelm the contrasting thunder of hilarity from the mess. "It's not like this every night," Mac assured Will. "Just a let-off of steam every now and again. And don't feel you have to put down a pint of whisky a day to be as good a pilot as Johnny. No one will think the worse of you if you stay sober."

Will felt a powerful urge to open his heart to this stalwart Scot, to tell him how tired and bewildered and ill he felt; and above all, to ask him if he had ever felt the pain of fear Will had experienced over the German trenches and felt again now at the thought of the next day's show. But, though his resolution was weakened by his weariness and the effect of the whisky, he managed to restrain himself. To show any sign of weakness must, he realized, undermine his own self-confidence as well as bring his courage into question.

As he lay down on his bed, with the hut circling gently and uneasily about him, he realized for the first time how trapped he was—trapped by himself. In a moment of defiance, or determination, he had set in motion the long series of events that had resulted in his being in a front-line scout squadron. From here, there was no escape. Technically, he could tell the major the next day that he was not going to fly, that he was underage, that he wished to be sent back to England. But that, of course, was unthinkable. He was now a part of this team; and the stark inevitability of the need to share with them these dangers—day after day, week after week—filled him with the same trapped fear that those two Germans must have experienced just before Johnny Watson tore their two-seater apart with his Vickers guns.

Will went to sleep almost at once, the last conscious image in his mind replaying the scene of the blazing ball of fire tearing toward the earth.

It was the wettest August in living memory, and the Allied armies, which had set out so hopefully at the end of July, were brought to a halt in the mud of Passchendaele. For the last weeks of the month, the two opposing armies occasionally bombarded each other and struggled to break free from the cloying mud. But the bursting shells only redistributed the smashed soil and killed a few thousand more troops, and no serious progress could be made on either side.

At Bildaut airfield, life was quieter than it had been for weeks. The day of Will's first show marked the end of the fine flying weather, and apart from a few abortive patrols, on which nothing was seen, the squadron remained on the ground. Will got permission to take up his Camel a couple of times. On one afternoon, he climbed straight up through the low cloud, and in clear blue sky, high above a blinding white cloud sheet that concealed the murk and the mud and the driving rain, he came to terms with the temperamental but endearing little scout. In mock combat with himself, he looped and stalled and spun and learned how you could put the Camel through a turn to the right that was so fast no marksman on earth, nor any known enemy scout, could hope to follow you. He began to love the Camel and to sense a growth of understanding between himself and this machine in which he would either soon die or become a successful war pilot.

At Bildaut, there was not much to do on the ground. Some of the more zealous pilots went over their Camels with their rigger and fitter, checking every wire and strut, the valve clearance of every cylinder; and with the armorer, stripped and assembled their machine guns with exquisite care. Then there was shooting and bombing at the local range, and aircraft recognition practice. But, for the most part, it was a dull time occupied with talk and games of bridge and chess and table tennis, with some impromptu indoor rugby in the mess after dinner. They began to feel slack from inaction, and on one wet afternoon, the major suddenly issued the shocking order that all officers below the rank of captain would put on shorts and run not less than two miles around the French countryside.

Will spent a lot of time with his machine and got to know the names of all the flight's riggers and fitters down in the big canvas hangars. He also began to feel that he had become a settled-in member of his hut. Mac was a good steadying factor against the wild temperament of Doug Raven, and Will became attached to Arthur Campbell, who was a true dreamy eccentric one moment and a fierce single-minded enthusiast the next. Fortunately, he was always in the second condition when he was flying. They made a good foursome in the hut; then Raven's promotion came through, and he went off to a hut of his own, and a new pilot called John Cole, five feet four inches tall and a mathematical wizard of all things, arrived to take his place. He was so good at chess that it no longer seemed worthwhile playing, but the little lad (he had to sit on a pile of engine manuals to see out of his Camel) did not take himself seriously, so that was all right.

The terrible weather continued into the first days of September. Then suddenly summer came back after all. Arthur Campbell stared gloomily into the low brilliant sun one morning and said, "A few more days to dry out, then we can all get on with the killing again. There was a t-t-time when the sun was an o-o-omen of renewed life and joy. N-n-now it means immi-imminent death by high explosive, a cylindrical piece of steel one third of an inch in diam-diameter, noxious gas in your eyes and lungs, or"—and he swung around gravely to the other three who were still in their beds—"or, in our case, by falling upwards of ten thousand feet through space, in or not in flames." After a pause he added, "I think I prefer the last of those fates."

Things were lively down at flight headquarters, and all sorts of rumors were rife: A new push was starting at once, and they would be back on ground-strafing; they were going to lay cinder runways on the grass so that they could carry bombs and not sink up to their bellies with the extra weight; the great German ace Manfred von Richthofen was out of hospital and back in action with his notorious Circus. Actually no machine could get into the air that day, as the ground was too waterlogged, but the next afternoon Mac told Will that he would be leading him and Arthur Campbell on an escort job at four o'clock.

They took off into a strong westerly wind in V formation, with Will concentrating very hard to maintain as tight a position as the much more experienced Campbell, and climbed straight up to ten thousand feet over the shattered remains of Ypres. They picked up the photographic F.E.2b, and Will felt renewed relief that he had got into a Camel rather than a Fee squadron. The Fee did not look much more formidable than a Rumpty, and the pilot and observer sitting in their pod ahead of the pusher engine looked like ready-made targets for the most inexperienced German machine gunner.

Their subflight of three Camels kept three thousand feet above the lumbering Fee, weaving from side to side to avoid getting ahead and to put off Archie, who was occasionally throwing up a few well-aimed bursts.

It was good clear photographing weather, and Will could see the Fee start on its run over some German rear positions. It was attracting a lot of Archie but was not able to take much avoiding action. Nasty work, thought Will. Then he saw Mac waggling his wings. He was pointing up toward the sun. Will had to look twice before he made out nine tiny dots. They were flying west in three V formations, but so strong was the wind that it looked as if they were stationary in the sky, like goshawks poised ready to drop on their victims.

Will saw three of them break from the formation and dive straight down. The black Archie blotches in the sky had neatly pinpointed the Camels for the German pilots, and Will knew that within a few seconds he would be facing combat for the first time.

A second trio had detached themselves and were following down the first, probably to attack the Fee the Camels were supposed to be protecting.

Their own position was an uncomfortable one, with odds against them. There was also something particularly unpleasant about the nature of these Germans. As they grew larger above them, they took on an entirely unfamiliar shape. At this angle, diving straight toward them, they looked more like complex box kites than scouts. They had three wings! Were they triplanes? Will had heard about a German scout with an entirely new configuration, and it was rumored that Richthofen himself had one. They were the newest German scout on the front and very splitarse indeed, so it was said.

At the last second before they came in, Mac signaled that he was going down to protect the Fee, and Campbell and Will were left to face the three triplanes alone. They were painted bright red and looked as if they would lose that ridiculous stack of wings if they turned sharply. But they had two nasty guns in the nose—and it was time, Will realized, to give serious attention now that one of them was less than a hundred yards away and steadying for a burst.

He gave his Camel full right rudder and pulled back hard on the stick so that he shot up into a tight climbing turn. At the same moment, he heard for the first time the ugliest sound known to a scout pilot, the *rat-a-tat-tat* of twin Spandau machine guns at close range, a decisive, metallic, and wicked note that could not possibly have any other purpose but the committing of death.

The burst went wide, the red triplane flashed past under Will's tail, and with the unmatched speed in a right turn that the Camel could accomplish, Will found himself with the German half filling his Aldis. He fired a quick burst and saw his tracer tearing into the triplane's tail. The damage did not appear to affect its agility. It slammed into a tight left-hand turn, almost standing on its wing tips. As Will followed it around, he was looking right into the German's cockpit, and he could see every detail—the Spandau breeches, the instruments, the pilot's gauntleted hand on the stick, even the shape of the pilot's face, a white oval beneath the helmet, the goggles adding to the effect of total hostility.

Nothing could outturn a Camel, he had been told many times, but as he pulled back harder on the stick in an effort to get in a full deflection burst, he realized his machine had met its match. Once he caught the triplane's slipstream, which made his Camel shoulder and threaten to spin out, then the red scout suddenly pulled up into a steep climbing turn. Will tried desperately to follow, but he was not nimble enough, and he watched it flick onto its back and drop away. He raced down after it, got in a short ineffectual burst at maximum range, and hurled himself into the melee below.

The triplane had left him to help finish off Campbell, who was fighting desperately against the other red scouts a thousand feet below. The flashing sequence of events that followed was too fast to assume any coherent shape. Will remembered tossing his machine into impossibly tight turns, shatteringly steep dives, and then up again, hanging on to his propeller, pushing forward the stick and giving hard rudder as yet another stream of Spandau tracers tore past his cockpit.

At one point, he was upside down, alone, looking straight down on the three triplanes buzzing in at poor Campbell from different directions. How any of them avoided collisions was beyond belief. As Will went down again with the wind screaming through his wires, he saw before him, at less than five hundred feet, the most appalling sight in air fighting.

He never saw how Campbell got in the burst, or even where he was, when one red triplane suddenly stood up on its tail, its engine smoking. It did not look badly hit; perhaps only one or two bullets had smashed into the engine. But a lick of flame followed the smoke and at once enlarged itself a hundred times into a frightful blue white configuration. Then out from the center of it there hurled the figure of the pilot, arms spread wide as if in appeal to the Deity. He had chosen the long, cool descent; it was better than death by fire. Turning gently over and over, still spread-eagled, the doomed pilot rapidly diminished in size until he was no more than a dot that faded to nothing.

Now there were suddenly many more machines in the sky. Wherever Will looked, he saw the glad sight of roundels. A flight of S.E.5s had come to their rescue, tearing after the retreating triplanes, and in a few seconds only Campbell and Will were left at the scene of the combat and one S.E.5, whose pilot waved cheerfully before climbing away to the east. There was no sign of Mac nor of the Fee.

Will could see that Campbell's machine was grievously damaged. The rudder was peppered through, one of the left ailerons looked smashed and inoperative, and the engine was leaving a trail of blue smoke. Will came up close alongside, and Campbell grinned across at him and held his nose between thumb and finger. Will could even see him blinking behind his goggles. Good old Arthur! Will thought. But, my God, what a sight he had made of that triplane!

It was hard going back toward the lines. The wind was as strong as ever, and they seemed scarcely to be moving. Archie was being troublesome, too, as he always was with a lame duck that could not take evasive action. The *whoomphs* got so close that Will made off and escorted Campbell from a safer distance.

There was still a mile to go before they crossed over the lines, when the puffs of blue smoke from Campbell's engine became a steady blue stream, then a black stream. Campbell switched off, fearful of fire, and went into a glide. He'll never make it, not against this wind, Will decided. Archie suddenly became frantic to cut him to pieces before he crash-landed, and as he dropped lower the machine guns joined in.

The Camel went steadily on. Will could make out its shadow, racing over the German rear trenches, growing larger at every yard as the machine dropped lower and lower. Just ahead was no-man's-land, a waste of mud and barbed wire and shell holes.

Will saw the Camel floating just above the ground, a frail helpless thing of wood and canvas facing the full tumult of modern war, touching down, rolling a few yards, violently somersaulting, and landing on its back like a squashed moth. At once, the German mortars opened up, plopping their shells in a closing pattern around the gray shape of the wrecked scout.

Will could wait no longer. His fuel was running short, and this was an especially unhealthy place. He sent up a silent prayer for Campbell, opened his throttle wide, and made for Ypres and thence to Bildaut.

He was shaking again, now that he was safe, and he hated himself for it. His body felt as if it were suffering the fever of a flu attack. He pushed up his goggles and wiped his face with the back of his gauntlet. My God, he confessed to himself for the first time, I didn't know it was going to be like this!

Mac landed just before him. As Will dropped down over Bildaut, he saw his Camel, with the single red streamer flying from its tail, taxiing in to the hangar. Mac was counting the holes in his fuselage when Will climbed down. "What happened to Arthur?" Mac asked. "Something dropped past in flames—was that him?"

Will gave him a brief summary of events, striving to sound matter-of-fact, and asked Mac how he had fared. "Aye, they got the Fee," he said in a dead voice. "I did what I could. I'll say one thing for those tripehounds, they're difficult to miss with all those wings. I put one of them to rest. But the other two sent down that poor wee Fee."

Mac shrugged his shoulders, and Will walked at his side away from the hangars. "This is a damn dirty war," Mac said. "We didn't grow up to do this sort of thing to one another. Let's have a drink and telephone Wing to see if they've got any news of Arthur."

The bar was already packed. A Flight was there in full strength, celebrating their flight commander's return from leave, and three of the S.E.5 pilots who had driven off the red triplanes had dropped in, short of fuel. Mac was in a strange black mood and seemed disinclined to talk. He put down two large whiskies in quick succession and then leaned his back against the bar and stared at the celebrating crowd with angry eyes. "You know what we are doing?" he asked. "We're living in a hothouse. There's nothing like a scout squadron to mature you fast. As far as learning the truth about this wicked world is concerned, we're compressing into a few months what we'd have needed six years to learn in peacetime. Ah well, as Robby Burns wrote,

> Man's inhumanity to man,
> Makes countless thousands mourn. . . .

He ordered two more drinks from the barman and raised his own glass. "But to quote Robby again, 'Freedom and Whisky gang thegither,' so here's to survival and freedom."

They drank in a corner of the bar, philosophizing intently. Will found himself watching the antics of his fellow officers with superior detachment induced by the whisky and the solemnity of Mac, for whom drinking, when it had to be done, was carried out as a national ritual. "There's a lot of mourning going on just now," Mac said. "Whatever happened to those two lads who arrived the day after you?"

Will had only spoken to them once. They had both filled gaps in A Flight, which had met an unlucky patch. One of them, called Gregory, had been shot down on his first job; the other one had done three shows, including some trench-strafing, and had then been seen diving away steeply to the east under suspicious circumstances. It would not have been the first time a pilot on either side had slipped away and landed behind the enemy lines for the sake of peace. "Poor laddie," Mac commented, shaking his head. "I wouldn't like to live with his conscience for the rest of my life."

Will thought about this and attempted a quick calculation in his mind between the discomfort of a lifelong conscience and the sharp agonies of fear this fighting business demanded. Perhaps, he wondered, you could come to terms with your own cowardice, and your conscience would eventually die of old age. He put it to Mac.

"In our curious situation," Mac replied slowly, "we have these two alternatives: Either we die and never find out, so the problem won't worry us. Or we live and learn the truth. If we are going to stay alive and sane—and Johnny Watson was only just sane when he left—we have got to use the scientific approach to this air fighting business. You agree there, laddie? Right . . ."

They went back to their favorite subject, morning, afternoon, or evening: the art of aerial combat. It was not only fascinating in itself. As their continued existence depended on their skill at this art, it was essential to give as much time as possible to developing it.

Just after midnight, all the sounds in the mess were drowned out by the noise of a revving motor bicycle engine outside. As it faded away into the night, the flap of the mess tent was pulled aside, and there, blinking in the bright light and swaying from side to side, was the tall thin figure of Arthur Campbell.

Will and Mac sprang up and caught him before he fell and lowered him into a chair. Everyone gathered around, demanding an explanation.

Campbell lifted his head and cast his glazed eyes around

the sea of curious faces. "I'm joining the infantry," he said in a thick voice, speaking slowly. "They really know how to throw a party. They go on, and on, and on . . ." And he lapsed into a deep sleep.

It was not until late the following morning that they succeeded in getting from Arthur Campbell a coherent account of what had happened. He had lain under his Camel in a shell hole for an hour until the Germans tired of machine-gunning and mortaring him. At dusk, a sergeant and a lieutenant had crept out across no-man's-land, and the three of them crawled back by slow stages. "Every few yards, they threw something at us—grenades, mortar bombs, or just p-p-plain b-b-bullets," Campbell told them. "Then we dropped down a long way into something they called the forward line. And the par-par-party started right there and went on all the way back to some dugout where there was a colonel who hadn't been sober for three days—so they said. Then I th-th-thought I ought to get back, so they put me on the back of a motorbike. Don't know how I hung on all the way here."

It was the last party for Campbell or any of them for more than two weeks. With the drying out of the ground after the August rain, the tempo of the ground fighting increased to a new crescendo, and this meant that the squadron was hard-pressed all day and on every day when the weather permitted. B Flight went up two and sometimes three times a day, escorting bombing raids by Martinsydes and D.H.4s, patrolling offensively and defensively against German scouts, and bombing and strafing German reinforcements, railway stations, and local infantry attacks. They saw few Germans in the air. The Germans were playing their usual tactics of patrolling behind their own lines and attacking only when their superiority in numbers or advantage of height made victory a near certainty. While

British photographic reconnaissance was carried out by slow and vulnerable planes that required an escort, the enemy sent over at a great height unescorted two-seaters for reconnaissance, with a performance as good or better than the scouts sent to attack them. By playing a defensive role, the German air service lost few aircraft, and few ever crashed behind the British lines. Time after time, Doug Raven led them after a German two-seater, but it was always too crafty and swift; and back on the ground, he would curse the cautious enemy, order his Camel to be refueled, and then get permission to go off on his own in search of prey. In this way, he got two balloons and a Rumpler, but his rigger was up half the night patching the holes in his machine.

As the weeks passed, Will noticed that his nerves were becoming toughened, his sensitivity blunted, by the daily round of danger and destruction. After six weeks on a scout squadron, he was past the worst of the danger period, it being an accepted statistic that every day of survival increased by a measure the chances of final survival. Week by week, the panorama of faces at dinner in the mess slowly changed. A lantern-jawed Australian in C Flight who had outlasted most of the rest of his flight was missing one evening; two more youngsters from C Flight whose names Will never learned disappeared in their first week; and little John Cole vanished into a cloud far over Germany, smoking badly, and Will hoped that his pocket chess set was safely tucked inside his right flying boot to help him fill the long hours if he was made prisoner.

Will had little time for the introspection and self-questioning that, he had long realized, had dogged his last weeks at school and had made harder his early days on the squadron. The need to walk alone or with an understanding companion, to escape from the noise of the mess and of airplane engines, disappeared with the opportunity to do these things. And his skin was hardening with the resolve to survive. Letters came regularly from his mother, and he read them with affection in his heart for her but with a feeling of total detachment from the events and people she wrote about. The world of Amplethwaite had seemed distant enough from southern England; now it had become a different planet altogether. All his contemporaries had left school at the end of the summer term and were either in the army or were about to join up. Tom Filton was a second lieutenant in the Lancashire Fusiliers, already in France, Will's mother believed. The vicar had been killed under circumstances of great gallantry.

The distance between Amplethwaite and the forward airfield of Bildaut on the western front narrowed momentarily as he read that the games would be taking place again this month as usual, that old Jim Appleton had taken first prize with his Herdwick ewe at Stonethwaite. But when he dropped the letter on his bed and looked out of the hut to see C Flight taking off in a flurry of sound with twenty-pound bombs, the dividing barrier between the past and the present slammed down again. His own flight would be following in less than an hour, on a deep patrol to clear the air for a big bombing raid on a German airfield. He viewed the imminent sequence of events dispassionately: the brusque briefing by Doug Raven; the starting procedure and the puff of blue smoke and whiff of burned castor oil as the Clerget burst into life; the brisk, almost perfunctory takeoff in two Vs; the sight of the landscape below turning from green to the pasty brown gray of the lines and back to green again in enemy territory; and, above all, the renewal of that spirit of shared danger and shared endeavor.

Mac did not say a word as they walked out to their machines. He was very quiet these days and even drank water with his dinner. But, before they separated, he paused and patted the tail of Will's Camel. "Watch this, laddie," he said. "It's going to be a long trip."

It was meant kindly but was an uncharacteristically alarmist thing to say, and it made Will feel faintly uneasy.

It was a fine October afternoon with broken clouds at five thousand feet, and they could see a vast distance, even as far as the shimmering strip of the English Channel to the northwest. The sky over Flanders was humming with activity. They caught a glimpse of a squadron of D.H.4s going out on a bombing raid, and below them, climbing for height as if intent on escorting them, Will saw a flight of Sopwith triplanes, as unbirdlike and improbable as their German counterparts but very handy for dogfighting, he had heard. A few minutes later, when they had reached ten thousand feet, he recognized by its swept-back wings a lone Rumpler, high above, on its way over to photograph behind the Allied lines. He pointed up to it, but Mac only shrugged his shoulders. They would never get near it with their rate of climb, and besides they had their own business to attend to.

Down below, somewhere the other side of Ypres, a great artillery barrage had just opened up, and even from this height they could see the torn ground quivering under the shock waves of the high explosive and the smoke drifting away in a gray polluting wave across the nearby undamaged countryside.

There were times when the war seemed to stand still for days on the western front, as if everyone had suddenly tired of it; then it would start up again with renewed ferocity, and the land and the air vibrated and seemed to be consumed by high explosive. Today was going to be a busy day for killing, Will could see. Archie showed himself full of venom the moment they crossed the lines, and my God how quick he was! The very first bursts were no more than fifty yards ahead, and a second later they were flying through the black-spreading smoke, catching whiffs of the high explosive. The next salvo came right below them, chucking about the sky Doug Raven's leading V, which was below and ahead of Mac's section. Raven altered course sharply to port and climbed a hundred feet to upset the German prediction.

But the next salvo slammed in right among them, the rapid sequence of the explosions sounding like a string of giant firecrackers; and the following pattern, no more than fifteen seconds later, was equally accurate. It was very rare for a scout to be hit badly by Archie at this height, but one of the flight was holed and began to fall away. It was their newest pilot, a fellow called Brummage, a farmer's lad from Shropshire, who had been flying number three to Raven. Will saw him swing out with his lower starboard wing flapping up and down. It tore away almost at once, and the Camel fell into an untidy spin. As the Camel's speed rose, other bits broke away, but it would be a long time before poor Brummage was put out of his agony. Will prayed that he would carry with him to the end some merciful fragment of hope that a miracle would occur and he would somehow pancake lightly, perhaps into water or a haystack. He disappeared rapidly from sight into a wisp of cloud. Their altitude mercifully shielded them from the sight of the violent end of one young life and one Sopwith Camel.

Then an odd thing happened. Will saw Doug Raven first wave to Mac to take over the flight and then dive down after the stricken Camel. Will guessed what he was going to do. It was sometimes almost impossible to resist the urge for revenge against those anonymous gunners, and this time Raven had yielded. He was going to try to locate the battery and shoot it up alone, a forlorn and desperately dangerous thing to do. For a flight commander, it was also highly irresponsible.

They had already lost one of their number, and now they were likely to lose two. Meanwhile, the remaining four Camels under Mac closed up and climbed to their operating altitude of fifteen thousand feet, still pursued by triumphant Archie bursts. It was wickedly cold. Will's teeth were chattering, and the shock of seeing Archie make a strike within a few yards of him, and the misery and anger this had caused left him feeling close to despair. He had survived nearly three months of this hideously dangerous war, and statistically he should have been dead long ago. He glanced at the other three Camels, rising and falling gently in the air alongside him, and wondered how Mac was feeling, and Arthur Campbell, and Vic Duncan, who had arrived a week after Will and appeared to have no nerves at all. All three were so resilient, Will thought, compared with himself.

His morbid brooding was shattered by the crackling sound of twin Spandaus from close behind, and the four Camels were instantly thrown into wild evasive action, climbing and turning like plovers caught on the wing. Will stabbed violently at his left rudder and hauled back his machine into a climbing turn, looking back for a glimpse of his assailant. An Albatros tore past above his head, a blur of red wings and black fuselage and undercarriage, the wheels seeming almost to graze his helmet.

They had been well and truly jumped from out of the sun, in spite of their vigilance. It was amazing how there was nothing to be seen in the sky, and a few seconds later, bullets were cutting into your fabric. Will had no time to count the Germans, but there were a lot of them about, all Albatros D.V.s, the latest and most feared of the breed.

The sky was already filled with twisting, turning, climbing, and falling machines as each pilot attempted to bring his sight to bear. The opening moves of a dogfight were governed by instinct and speed of response. There was no time for planning. Will thought he saw Mac a few hundred feet below with two Albatroses on his tail and another hovering above, but he was unable to go to his rescue. Another was sticking tightly behind his own tail, and Will had to use all the agility of the Camel to keep out of the tracers' killing line. He pulled back savagely on the stick, deliberately stalling his machine, and kicked her into a spin. He was out of it again almost before he had completed a revolution, and with his engine screaming at full revs he tore into the melee below.

He had been right. Mac was in real trouble. There were now four Albatroses making passes at him as he circled almost on his wing tips. Will caught one of them with a full deflection shot. It flicked up and over his head, the black-helmeted pilot clearly visible. Then there was a second one in his sight, momentarily flying straight and level. The range was too great, but Will was by now a good shot, and he saw his tracers smashing into the Albatros's tail. The German began to turn, but it was a scrappy halfhearted maneuver, perhaps handicapped by the damaged tail. With twenty degrees of deflection on his Aldis, Will pulled the firing ring again for a long burst. He could see that he was hitting everything—the cockpit, the engine, the fuel tank, and the upper wing surface again and again. He swung his Camel under the doomed Albatros, up the other side in a climbing turn that allowed him to see into the cockpit at close range. The pilot, sprawled forward, was either dead or unconscious, and his machine fell forward under the pressure of the stick to a vertical power dive.

The dogfight had spread out across the sky. Mac was half a mile away and slightly below, still struggling with a single Albatros, and there was more fighting going on above. A machine detached itself in a long straight glide, laying a long line of black smoke. It was another Albatros.

Good God, they were not only holding their own but swatting them out of the sky! Will clawed his way upward, light with elation and thirsting for more. They would get the lot of them, the whole damn *Jasta*! He could see Arthur Campbell in the midst of a milling mass of red sharp-nosed machines. There must have been five of them after him. Will got in a long burst at maximum range and hit nothing before his guns jammed. He struck the breeches in turn with his fist, pulling the firing ring, and they worked. Quick cure!

An Albatros was heading straight for him in a shallow dive, and Will turned to meet it head-on. They both held their fire in this fearful test of nerves until it seemed as if they must crash nose to nose. Flashes of flames were coming from above the German's spinner, and Will got in a quick burst before they both turned, to left and right, belly to belly, in a blur of scarlet and olive drab. Will flicked upward, turned sharply in the reverse direction, and looked behind, above, and to each side.

The sky was empty of the enemy. There was not a red machine to be seen. It was incredible how the Germans came from nowhere and disappeared to nowhere seemingly without any warning. This was how the enemy liked to fight: to come in swiftly, to make several diving attacks using superior speed and climb, and to destroy as much as they could. They were gone as soon as they had done their damage or when things became too dangerous.

The reason why they had left so early and hastily in this dogfight could be seen far below, where a tall spire of smoke rose from the middle of a field. There was at least one more pile of shattered remains down there. But the Camel Flight was still intact: Mac five hundred feet above and signaling them to join him; Arthur Campbell a mile away to the north; and Vic Duncan, grinning with triumph, was already close formating on Will.

They flew back through a veritable black curtain of Archie hate—the word seemed to get around every battery when revenge was called for—and over the lines at ten thousand feet, switching to gravity tanks as their fuel ran low. The setting sun into which they flew home took on an appropriately bloodier hue, and the storm clouds rearing up high about it were like scarlet-outlined giant gravestones. When Will cut his engine for the glide in, he could already hear the growling of the guns opening their nightlong strafe.

It had been a real day of war—the hate, the fear, both unremitting; an ugly day, shot through with moments of awful fear and awful elation. When Will climbed out, he found that his legs would not support him. He collapsed forward over the lower wing, arms spread wide, his eyes closed. He knew he wanted to be sick, but shame helped him to fight it off. He opened his eyes to find himself staring at a ragged tear in the canvas, and his fitter, dear old Nobby Clark, had an arm across his shoulder. "Are you all right, sir?" he asked.

Will pulled himself up and began to draw off his gauntlets. "Yes, fine, Nobby. A bit tired, that's all. It was a long show, and we had a bit of a scrap. Did Captain Raven get back?"

"Yes, sir. But I can't think how. You take a look at his bus, sir."

Will walked over to the hangar and found Raven's Camel. He had never seen anything like it. It was peppered through and through with holes, one aileron had disappeared, a tire was punctured, and the windshield was shattered. But this was the minimum price you paid for attacking an antiaircraft battery; it was usually higher.

Doug Raven was in the bar, unrepentant at leaving them, and filled with a dour satisfaction at the vengeance he had wreaked. He had heard of their scrap, of the two Albatroses they had shot down and the three more they had damaged, and he congratulated them and set up great drinks for everyone. But like a man who has survived a major operation for a fatal disease, he could talk of little else but his own escape. The long pent-up hatred of the men who sent those diabolically dangerous and accurate shells into the sky had exploded in that wrathful dive and the strafe that had followed it. "Honor satisfied, honor satisfied," he kept muttering as the drinks went around again. "You should have seen those buggers run and tumble over as I drilled them. There was one machine-gun crew who wouldn't duck when I went for them. They thought they'd got me. Nearly did, too. But, the third time I went in, I held the old bus until the prop nearly carved up their gun barrel. That silenced them all right—and me," he added with a caustic laugh.

It would have been a bigger party if the major had not come in, full of smiles but also with the warning that the whole squadron was on early call. "Something big on," he added darkly.

Something big, Will said to himself caustically, repeating the words. Something big. For God's sake, what was today, then? Dead young men in the sky, at least one killed by himself. Dead young men on the ground, dozens of them killed by Doug Raven. Hundreds, maybe thousands more killed here on the western front by shell, bullet, bayonet, poison gas . . . Was today a "something small" day? Then what did tomorrow—"something big"—hold for them?

After dinner, Will felt that he had to get into the open air, and he slipped out of the big tent to face the booming autumnal darkness. The horizon was flashing white as it had been on the night of his arrival. He had been shocked by Doug Raven's performance, and he wanted to clear himself of its influence on his mind. Normally there was no element of relish in what they had to do. To kill was a rotten business, only a little less rotten than being killed yourself. But it was this margin that kept them fighting for all they were worth, and meanwhile there was a certain tradition that had to be followed in order to keep the rottenness down to a minimum.

The German was a German, a brave, skillful, and probably decent enough fellow. And to keep the fighting as nearly as possible on the level of a highly competitive game, the score was all-important. Today Will had got an Albatros, not a twenty-year-old boy with fair hair from Bavaria whose mother treasured his letters and tomorrow would be mourning him. This was the only way to keep your nerve, even your sanity. This, and a strong team spirit, and a generous nightly dose of alcohol.

Like most scout pilots, Will had unconsciously built up a defensive network against the stresses of combat life. It was a delicate thing that had often been sorely tested, especially after several days of unpleasant jobs when Archie seemed to be splitting the sky about you, and Pfalzes, Fokkers, and Albatroses seemed to lurk behind every cloud, and there were empty places in the mess at dinner. But that evening, the structure was at breaking point, and Will faced with aching apprehension another heavy day. The mechanics would be working all through the night to repair their machines. Soon after dawn, the first flight would go out, and it would be a trench-strafe, and Will's life would hang on the statistics of probability of some unknown German machine gunner anticipating the Camel's sharp evasions, selecting the correct deflection, and pulling the trigger.

He opened the door of his hut. The curtains had not been drawn, but by the intermittent light from the artillery fire, he could see that all four beds were unoccupied, three of them with the sheets turned back by the batmen, the flying gear neatly laid out, the heavy leather coats on hooks. Once again, for the third time since Will had joined the squadron, the fourth bed was stripped back, awaiting a replacement.

They had hardly known Brummage. A silent lad, he had been with them for only a week. He had lived with his sister, which was rather curious, in a village near Wellington, and they shared a small farm. That was about all they had learned. He had had big hands, Will remembered, perhaps too coarse for the gentle art of controlling a Camel. But the most delicate touch could not have saved him today. Will, resting with his back against the closed door, his hand tightly clutching the handle, thought about Brummage's long last journey down, watching the breakup of the frail structure of his shattered Camel.

He thought next about the unnamed man he had killed and the unnamed man who had tried to kill him. A series of faces, of men who were still with the squadron, others who had left, and more who had died since Will had arrived at Bildaut, all passed before his eyes.

He was shaken from his condition of strained preoccupation by a sudden twist of the handle he was holding. "What in blazes?" a voice was calling out from the other side of the door. "Hey, Will, are you in there?"

Will spun around and opened the door, his mind groping for an excuse. He could see only the faint outline of the face in the dim light, but he knew it was no one from his squadron.

"Come on, Will Thompson, Lieutenant R.F.C., knight of the air, toast of the girls of Amplethwaite, you know who I am—Hugh Sanderson."

Will reeled back into the hut and steadied himself. "This is wonderful," he said at last. "What are you doing here?"

"You mean here in your jolly dormitory? Digging you out for a nightcap. And why I'm at Bildaut I'll tell you on the way to the bar."

They walked rapidly back to the mess together, with Hugh Sanderson doing the talking, telling Will that he had been back at the front for a month, that he had his own flight, and that they had just got rid of their Pups for S.E.5s. "Marvelous buses. We've really got the Hun licked with them."

In the light of the mess, Will felt reassured by the sight of the cheerful face and the clear blue eyes of his old friend. The directness of his speech, the straight simplicity of his mind, were equally reassuring.

"I hear you knocked one down today," Sanderson said admiringly. "That's good, very good. Knew I'd backed a winner." He offered Will a cigarette, then looked at him more closely and critically. "But you don't look too well. It's a rough game all right, but don't let it get you down. And don't fly tomorrow unless you're in top form. Stupid thing to do. It's going to be a hard day."

Will understood the reason for Sanderson's cautioning advice a few minutes later, when he heard that every machine that could fly would be out at first light, working independently on a narrow sector of the front, right back to the reinforcement areas, bombing and shooting up any target they could find. It was desperately important to stem a threatened German counterattack. Hugh Sanderson had come over from a nearby airfield to represent his squadron in a joint tactical discussion. The air would be thick with machines—more than one hundred in all—and the Germans would fill the air, too, with shot and shell.

The mess remained crowded, but the noise and the drinking had diminished. Hugh Sanderson found a table in the corner, and they talked over a bottle of Vichy water about the months since they had last met. Will listened to his account of how he had persuaded the hospital to release him while his leg was still in plaster and how he had actually flown with his bad leg strapped to the side of the cockpit and a hand control for the right rudder bar. "But no squadron would have me, the fools," he added, "and it wasn't until September that I got in with this lot. But worth waiting for. Good squadron, and I've got a good flight."

They discussed the relative merits of the S.E. and Camel, and Sanderson launched into a long and detailed analysis of the surest way of shooting down a two-seater: how to get on to his blind spot, where to aim for, how to get clear before the observer could bring his gun around on you. Will did his best to listen carefully and to ask intelligent questions, for this was an important lesson he was listening to, but the same scenes that had filled his mind in the darkness of the hut kept returning, however hard he attempted to reject them. And with each scene, like the caption in a silent movie, there appeared the words *Honor satisfied!*

It was nothing to do with honor. It was simple old-fashioned butchery, in the air and on the ground. And they would be at it again tomorrow, and the next day, day after day. It wasn't possible to keep going any longer. He was breaking up.

Hugh Sanderson was holding a packet of cigarettes in one hand to represent a Rumpler; the box of matches in the other was the attacking scout. Will watched his face as he maneuvered the two machines. "Now you've got him," he announced triumphantly and imitated the sound of a machine gun. He was as cheerful as if he had just won a set of tennis.

He finished his glass and got up from the chair. "It's going to be a short night. I must go. I think it's time you got transferred to my flight, Will. We'd finish the war in a week!"

The cheerfulness, simple optimism, and self-confidence of Hugh Sanderson lingered in the corner of the mess after he had gone, and when Will left for the second time, accompanied by two other B Flight pilots, he felt less depressed and less uneasy. But he slept badly that night. The German bombers were out in strength, shaking the hut and filling the air with the sound of their engines, and the boom of the guns rose and fell. The crescendo of the new push was matching the crisis point of Will's own fever, and toward dawn the effects of Hugh Sanderson's dose of medicine seemed to be wearing off.

Will waited for the daylight, his eyes open, staring at the gray square of the window against the blackness. He heard the approaching steps of the batman, like a jailer on the day of execution, and watched the door open softly. The man drew the black curtains across the window and went in turn to the three beds, pausing uncertainly for a moment by the fourth until he remembered that it was empty again. "Time to get up, sir," he said, with a hand on Will's shoulder. "The hot water is in the basin."

Except for a few complaining groans, they dressed in silence. Mac rarely cursed, but he expressed all their feelings when he said, "What a sod of a day!"

Arthur Campbell was coughing and spluttering while he tried to shave. He had had a cold for several days, and he was obviously much worse. "It's fil-fil-filthy f-f-flu, that's what it is."

"Get back to bed, then," Mac said sharply. "You won't be able to see a thing, and you'll probably fly into my tail."

Campbell did not bother to reply, and Mac and Will both knew that he would insist on flying, especially since they had been told of the importance of every machine getting into the air that day.

The batman brought them cups of scalding coffee, and they hurried down to the flight. The major was there in his flying gear, always confirmation that there was a crisis on. In the predawn half-light, he was talking to the three flight commanders beside his own Camel, a very clean bus with a red-painted engine cowl.

The mechanics were having their busiest time for weeks, and there was a great deal of activity in front of all the hangars. Will saw the flight sergeant walk up to Doug

Raven after the major's briefing was finished. The noise of the major's engine being warmed up drowned out the man's words, but Raven was evidently not pleased and was gesturing violently as he hurried into a hangar with the flight sergeant. A moment later, Will saw an airman emerge from the hangar and come running across the grass toward him. "Captain Raven would like to see you, sir."

"I know you've had a hard night of it, flight," Will heard Doug Raven saying. "But you know what our orders are—to get every damn machine into the air—somehow." He caught sight of Will. "Your bus is u.s.," he said. "They couldn't finish it after the pasting you gave it yesterday. So you'd better get back to bed."

Will was almost overwhelmed by a flood of conflicting emotions—of blessed relief and the joy of living another day, of unease because this was a cheat, of deprivation because he would never know how he would have stood up to the hazards of this big show, of suspicion that someone had thought his nerve was breaking and had arranged this.

He knew he ought to be cursing his bad luck or making some light remark about catching up on his sleep. Instead Will found himself saying, "I'd better take Campbell's bus, sir. He's got flu and a raging temperature. He's quite unfit to fly."

Will set the fine adjustment and taxied out after Mac. There was still hardly enough light to take off, the clouds were low, and a light drizzle was falling. It was impossibly dangerous bombing and strafing weather. Arthur Campbell had made a terrible fuss, and in the end the major had had to order him back to bed. Lucky old Arthur! And this was a good bus, thought Will, as he lifted the Camel lightly off the ground. Even with four bombs under her belly, she felt like a nice self-confident machine, well set-up for killing the enemy.

The plan was to go out in subflights of three and split up over the lines, but it was difficult to hold any sort of formation under these bumpy conditions, and at nine hundred feet they were scraping the bottom of the cloud. Canadian troops had helped to capture Passchendaele, and the R.F.C.'s business was to attack the enemy before he could counterattack. Mac took them low over the brown devastated strip that had once been the front line, and signaled the formation to break up when the ruins of Passchendaele loomed into sight through low-flying mist and the smoke of battle.

Will pulled away to the right and relaxed from the responsibility of formation flying. He was on his own now, to bomb and strafe his way into his own private war; to be fired at by every gun the Germans could bring to bear on his Camel; or to get lost deliberately on the safe side of the lines or fly back to his airfield with supposed engine trouble, as some pilots were known to do.

It was impossible to distinguish what was going on only a hundred feet below. The blasted trees, the crater-pitted fields, the dead horses, the shell of a farmhouse, the occasional figure, lurking and half-concealed, told of nearby combat. But as always it was the untidiness and the shapelessness of the picture that predominated. Up here, it was all clear-cut. You were friend or foe by the roundel or black cross painted on your machine, and you shot at an enemy you could see instead of anonymously mass-killing by gas or high explosive half a dozen miles away.

Will knew he was over the front line only by the tracer that began to flash up toward him. From unseen muzzles, it began its flight lazily, seemingly harmless and easily avoidable, and became hostile only at close range before whipping past at a ferocious speed. Will felt the familiar dryness in his mouth and began to throw his Camel about the sky, at the same time searching for a target.

Get rid of your bombs; that was the first thing to do. There was nothing worthy of them, only a few freshly dug trenches. He pushed the Camel's nose down and began hedgehopping farther behind the German lines and suddenly saw a heavy artillery battery ahead. He was lucky to have chanced on it and sharp-eyed to have spotted it through its camouflage nets. The ground fire intensified as he turned straight for the center, but he had to hold his machine steady for a few seconds. Alarmed figures were scattering, others were snatching rifles from their shoulders. He grazed over the ugly elevated barrel of the first gun, dropped his nose, and pulled the bomb release.

The Camel lifted in relief at the loss of weight and at once became more spirited. Now he could splitarse without any worries. He kicked the rudder pedals to swing the arc of his guns over a wide area and pulled the firing ring for a long burst, went into a sharp turn, and raced away as fast as he could go. He turned in his seat just in time to see the seven-second fused bombs send up a mighty column of brown soil. At least he had unsettled them and killed a few.

A minute later, he saw a train. Luck was laying on the targets for him this morning. He climbed to get a better perspective and was greeted at a hundred feet by an onslaught of Archie of every kind. It must be a very special train to be so cherished by the Germans. Will looked longingly at the line of freight cars, tightly packed with a load concealed by tarpaulins. He should have kept his bombs for this. But he must give it one run with his Vickers.

Will never got his Aldis on to that inviting target. A

burst of machine-gun fire cut sharp and clean into the nose of his Camel. Two bullets smashed into the breeches of his Vickers; another tore one side of the windshield off its mounting so that it swung around in the slipstream, allowing a tornado of wind to tear against his face; and a fourth drove into his left foot.

He was so shocked and affronted by the sudden success of the gunners that he was not conscious of his injury for some seconds. Then he was suddenly more frightened than he had ever been in his life, less of the pain and even of the crash and the death that might ensue than of the crippling effect this must have on his ability to fly and evade the fire that was now even more intense.

The engine was running sweetly, and the Camel could still climb. To streak away at low level without the delicate control of the rudder was to invite disaster, so Will pulled back hard on the stick, pursued by the hateful black blots of heavy Archie shell burst. The low ceiling, which they had cursed before takeoff, was now his salvation, and the damp tendrils of cloud wrapped about him, first cutting off part of the earth below, then mercifully swallowing the Camel whole.

A minute later, he came out into blinding sunshine and a limitless white ocean, the lonely world outside the world, explored only by those who braved the hazards of cloud flying. He had it to himself, but there was no joy in it for him. With the end of the need to concentrate on escaping and flying, the pain from his smashed foot hit him in convulsive waves. What was left of his boot was full of blood, and he felt a detached sense of pity for his foot, as if it were a beloved animal in a piteous condition. He tried to move it to catch a glimpse of the injury, and the wave of agony almost made him faint.

Concentrate on flying, Will told himself. You've got to get back. Get back. Before you lose too much blood. Before you pass out.

Plucky, lucky Camel. She was behaving spiritedly, and the engine was as healthy and strong as it had been at takeoff. Sopwith Pup, Sopwith Camel. What wonderful little flying machines! Will found himself talking to his Camel like a friend who had saved his life. "You're a real goer, little Camel, aren't you? The Hun can't get you even if he's put a bullet in my foot. Despite all that Archie and machine-gun and rifle fire—you avoided the lot didn't you? Or nearly the lot. But your heart's beating as strongly as ever, the Clerget rotary's rotating, the prop's spinning."

Then Will turned on himself fiercely. "Stop all this chatter. If you're going to survive—if you're ever going to see Vicky again—you'd better concentrate on flying and getting your beloved little Camel home, with you in the cockpit—and before you pass out."

Will got on to a northwesterly course, with the low sun right behind him, and decided to fly like this for ten minutes and drop back through the cloud. A gap would have been a comfort, to check his position and offer him visual descent. For he was in a real fool's paradise up here, with no means to check the depth of cloud and no instruments to help him through.

He put the Camel's nose down. The gray flecks streamed past the wing tips, and it became darker again as the sun was lost and the cloud swallowed him. He soon lost all sense of balance and direction, and it was not until he felt his body tightening against his strap that he realized he must be diving steeply. He pulled back hard on the stick until it began to go slack in his hands. He was already in a stall, probably on his side too. This was ridiculous. He forced the stick forward again, close to panic, straining for a glimpse of the sunless landscape he knew was below.

Then the light suddenly increased. Out of the side of the cockpit, there was a splash of green at an impossible angle. The glimpse was all he needed to reorientate himself. He was diving at forty-five degrees, almost on his side, and the ground was coming up too fast. He pulled over and back on the stick to bring the Camel straight and level at about two hundred feet and began to search for landmarks. A railway line going north without a bend. A hamlet on his right, only partly destroyed. An unevenly shaped wood. A lake. The lake was the clue. It was harp-shaped, the sharper end pointing toward Bildaut.

Landing with only right rudder was going to be interesting. He tried moving his right foot to the left rudder bar, kicked his injured leg, and shouted out with the agony. There was Bildaut. Dear old Bildaut. Scene of so many parties. So many tragedies and absences. So many emotions for Will. Bewilderment, anxiety, satisfaction, fear of fear, fear of disgrace. Last night, he had been near the end. Today he might have been put on that list—unfit for flying duties. Ultimate shame. But he hadn't. He could have been honorably in bed, but he had bullied his way into the air.

So no self-accusations, please, because there would be none from anyone else. Damn it, he had fifty jobs in his logbook, and today he had bombed a battery when he needn't have risked his neck. And now he had a blighty wound, all right. This time it was more than a twisted ankle. An honorable wound. No limping away down the fell, searching his conscience and finding it wanting and losing lovely Vicky. Now it was peace and quiet, clean sheets, caring nurses.

But first he had to get down. And, oh God, he was

getting weak. He flew in on his stick, with occasional dabs with his left rudder. He was finding it difficult to read the airspeed indicator, and sometimes the grass appeared close by, sometimes quite a long way away. He must pay attention and get his focus right.

"Come on, little Camel. Don't let me down now—even if I'm not flying you as well as you deserve. It's only because I've got a bad foot—I wonder if they'll have to take it off. A cripple for life . . ." This sudden, new speculation struck him like another Mauser bullet. Will Thompson never walking properly again—the fell runner unable even to walk!

Will almost lost consciousness on the landing glide. Instinctive corrections derived from long practice saved him. Considering the bumpy conditions, it was a very good landing. The Camel rolled along, almost straight, for about fifty yards, and went into a gentle ground loop, ending up facing the direction from which it had come, as if to say "Here you are, I've brought you home," and then turning to give a bow for the applause.

Only when Will failed to taxi in to the hangars did anyone realize that there was something wrong. Then the ambulance crew started its engine and bumped across the field to the stationary Camel. Will had fallen forward, and his head rested between the breeches of the twin Vickers machine guns. They pulled him out gently, down onto the lower wing and onto a stretcher. They applied an emergency tourniquet to his leg and drove away fast for the field hospital at Archoix, two miles away.

There were three others in the ward, in the hospital back in England. They were infantry officers and, with Will, they made a cheerful foursome. All of them had served long enough to have become sickened of the squalid filth, the noise, and danger of life on the western front, and unashamedly welcomed the respite they had gained, even if they might be limping for the rest of their lives or crippled with arthritis in middle age. For men like these, who had proved that they could withstand the strains and in months had become canny veterans, there was little glory left in the war. They had become cynical realists. As one of them put it to Will on his morning of arrival from France: "I've had nine months of it—now it's somebody else's bloody turn."

For the first few days, Will was less cheerful than the others. He was desperately worried about the state of his ankle, and he had nightmares about having his foot amputated. He had been assured that this would not be necessary, but during the day he would lapse into periods of melancholy, remembering how he had been able to race up the fells as fast as anyone his age, enjoying the speed and the filling of his lungs and the coordination of his muscles. He would never run like that again.

The other officers had all been through this period of gloomy introspection. On the third morning, one of them —a captain named Pellew, who had lost a leg at Ypres in early October—had thrown a copy of *The Times* at Will and told him to look at the Killed in Action and Missing lists. "Count up those and then count your luck," he said tersely. Then they had a game of rummy, and Will felt better.

That afternoon, the door of their ward was pushed open by a crutch, and the figure of Haddow appeared. "Hullo, Will," he said. His brown hair, parted in the middle, was brushed back, and on his face there was an expression of delight at their mutual recognition. He sat down, his right leg stretched out stiffly, and dropped his crutches on the floor.

"I heard you left hospital months ago," Will said.

"So I did. And here I am back again. I heard there was an R.F.C. chap in the place, and it turns out to be you. Good! You remember we once talked about ourselves as Ford cars turned out on the production line. Well, I'm that dud model that everyone forgot to check. Accident-prone. First of all, I knock myself against you and nearly kill us both, then I'm put together again and up I go in my Fee, and my engine conks out and the nearest field is too far, so I drop into a ratted glasshouse." His freckled face broke into a world-weary smile. "Don't throw stones in glass-houses, and don't fly into them. No, it's back to the trenches for me when this lot's healed up."

Haddow entertained them all for half an hour and had tea with them. His spritely cynicism made them all laugh, and Will recognized that he would be striking the wrong note if he claimed that the blame was his for that crash at Higher Training.

When a nurse took away their tea, Haddow said, "Aren't they marvelous? But the best of the lot went yesterday. I asked her to marry me as she walked into the ward for the first time. She came from your part of the world, too, somewhere in Westmorland."

Will's look of anguish caused Haddow to change his tone. "What's the matter, does she belong to you?"

"What was her name?" Will asked. He had heard from his mother that Vicky had finished her training in September. It was just possible.

"Nurse Mason I think it was. But I always called her Vicky. She's gone to a hospital in France, somewhere near Doullens."

"She used to belong to me," said Will, and, to his relief, Haddow did not pursue the subject.

Haddow had gone by the time Will himself was on crutches. He prayed that Haddow would somehow survive. Two of the beds in the ward emptied and were filled again, and he began to feel like an old-timer. His ankle was healing well, and the doctors were pleased with him.

Until a Sunday early in December, his life seemed to have fallen into the most uneventful phase he had ever experienced. He was not even in much pain anymore. Then on a Saturday morning, he received a letter. It was stamped Passed by Censor and was obviously from France. The single sheet was typed. It was from the major. In formal but friendly terms, it told him that his promotion had come through and that he had been awarded the Military Cross.

At first when he read the news, Will was filled with indignation. He had done nothing to deserve this. You didn't get an M.C. for being scared every time you went up. They were just sorry for him for being wounded. And what about Mac? Now *there* was a real pilot, steady, responsible yet brave as a lion.

But Mac had his M.C. too. In the last paragraph, the major told him that the awards had been made for that scrap with the Albatros and, in Will's case, also for temporarily putting out of action a German heavy battery, which had helped to repulse the counterattack. After this, Will felt better. He did not deserve the award, of course, but he began to feel a sense of satisfaction that he had—alone and by his own skill—altered by one minute of one degree the course of history.

Will was let out for Christmas. The doctors had not yet finished with him, and he was to be on crutches for another two months, but his bones had set well, and the deep wound across his ankle had healed. He was driven in an ambulance all the way to London and was left to make his own way to the platform at Euston station.

There was a light snow falling, and the station was brightened by patriotic Christmas decorations. Will watched the ambulance drive off and remembered the time, just thirteen months ago, when he had made his way out of this same station in his only suit, with a few pounds in his pocket and apprehension in his heart. All because of a slip, he told himself sorrowfully, and a pretty face. And now what? What had those thirteen months done to him?

Before he had time to consider this, he heard a voice beside him say, "I'd like to carry your bag for you, sir, if I may." Will turned and faced an elderly man in a high-winged collar, a bowler hat, and an astrakhan-collared black overcoat: a distinguished city gentleman anxious to do his bit and help a war hero. Will was filled with shame and at the same time was conscious of the figure he made standing in the snow, in R.F.C. uniform, his open greatcoat revealing the M.C. ribbon sewn beneath his wings, and supported on crutches. He must play the part.

"That's very good of you, sir," said Will. "All the porters seem to have gone to the front." He followed the man into the station, embarrassed at the situation and at the silence they seemed unable to break. The businessman placed the case on the rack and raised his hat. "God bless you, boy," he said, and paced away briskly down the platform before Will could say a word.

The last taxi to survive the gas shortage was awaiting Will at Windermere station. The driver might have been conducting royalty and did not unbend until they had crossed in the lake ferry from Bowness. "You'll get a bit of a surprise at the other end, young sir," he said darkly. "This is a big day for the Amplethwaite folk."

It was worse than Will had feared. In spite of the cold and the late hour, half the pupils of Amplethwaite Private were waiting under the command of Mr. and Mrs. Venner, who had, rather curiously, put on their Sunday best as if this were a funeral procession.

Will was at the mercy of the driver, who halted outside the gates. The children, led by the Venners, began to sing "Hail the Conquering Hero" and, at the end, waved many Union Jacks. Jim Shore's youngest sister, aged five and with her pigtails tied in red, white, and blue ribbons, stepped forward with a bouquet.

Will wanted desperately to sink back into the darkest recesses of the taxi, to hide from the admiring villagers, and to think of one who was not there, the one he half wanted desperately to see and yet was fearful of meeting again after all this time and after all they had been through. Oh, Vicky! Once *my* Vicky! Amplethwaite was not Amplethwaite without Vicky Mason.

But Will knew that he must respond to this generous, kindly intended welcome. He forced himself to lean out of the window and wave his forage cap. Prunella Shore handed him the flowers and fled, and Will said, "Thank you all very much. I'm afraid I don't deserve it, but thank you all the same. I'm sorry I can't get out, but it's a bit of a business with this leg."

He heard a murmur of sympathy and, in his best lieutenant's voice, ordered the driver to take him home.

There was a banner strung across the road outside the post office. WELCOME TO OUR HERO it said, and someone had rather inaccurately embroidered a pair of R.F.C. wings under the message.

A lot of people he knew were standing outside their houses, and he waved back as the driver proceeded slowly up the road. There were twenty or thirty more outside his own house. His mother broke from the crowd and ran forward to the taxi before it stopped. The tears were pouring down her cheeks.

"Oh, Will, Will," his mother kept repeating. "What a day! What a day!" She pulled the crutches through the door and handed them to his father, calling irritably, "Hold them, Dad."

Will hoisted himself out and stood on one leg. He could not recognize all the faces in the dusk. They looked like pale balloons bobbing about in a breeze, but he knew he had to smile and wave a hand in greeting.

"Thank you, everybody." It was all he had to say and all that was expected of him. They were singing "For He's a Jolly Good Fellow," and when they had finished, he heard his mother say sharply, "That's enough now. The lad needs to come in and rest." To make amends, his father said, "Bless you for coming along. Good night."

The sitting room was like the hospital ward after visitors' day, and his mother had lit four kerosene lamps to illuminate to the best advantage the dozen or more bowls of flowers. There was a huge bunch from Lord Lonsdale and one almost as large from Vicky's parents. Will stared about in wonder while his mother held him around his shoulders, half in support, half in affection and relief.

"Let the lad sit down," said his father. There was a bottle of whisky on the table, something they rarely had in the house. "I'm told this is what they like in the R.F.C.," he said. He poured out a large measure, and Will noticed that his hand was shaking. "You must have some, too, Mother. We've got to toast our Will."

As his father raised his glass, the bouquet of the whisky brought to Will's mind a bewildering sequence of faces. There was Henry Nicholls, bent over the bar, with his soiled cap in front of his glass, wiping his unkempt mustache, ramming home his points with a black-nailed finger. He saw Johnny Watson, close to the breakup of his nerves, reaching forward angrily for his first midmorning double. And Doug Raven, breathing hellfire and hatred for the Germans, setting up the glasses of the rich brown liquid to steady himself and his pilots after a filthy trench strafe.

"God bless you, Will, my brave boy." It was his mother who gave the toast. Bother it all, she was crying again!

Upstairs in his bedroom on the windowsill, carefully dusted by his mother, stood the model airplane, the half-completed memorial to a half-forgotten age. He picked it up tenderly. It was not bad. One day, when the war was over, he would finish it and send it with a letter to Hugh Sanderson, if they were both still alive.

Will longed to get up on the fells, to hear the music of the becks, see again the tumbling outline of Black Crag against the winter sky and feel the crisp winter bracken under his feet. For the first two days after his homecoming, ice and thin-lying snow made it impossible to go more than a few steps on his crutches. On Christmas Day, a thaw set in, and he went off after the big midday Christmas dinner when his mother and father were both asleep.

It was heavy going up the stone-strewn bridle track, and he often had to rest. He sat on a boulder close to the spot where he had started his practice runs. He looked up at the sky where he had seen Hugh Sanderson racing down the valley in his Pup, waving cheerfully before disappearing from sight. There were only two rooks now, wheeling about and diving in pursuit of each other. It might have been a dogfight between a Camel and a Fokker, but Will dismissed the similarity almost as soon as it came to his mind. All that was over for now, the fury and the fear. He was at peace in the world he loved.

Old Dove came down from the fellside, carrying an injured ewe, his collie at his heels. He nodded at Will in his familiar way as he passed, muttering something about the weather, and walked on, stalwart and steady as if he had last seen Will yesterday. Will found that to be the most comforting thing that had happened since his return.

In the evening, Vicky's younger sister arrived with a message—a message that brought back more than the words of the girl: "Mum says will you please come to tea tomorrow." It reawoke the memory and the reality of Vicky herself, the pain of which, like the pain of his ankle, was beginning to fade.

Will gained time by fetching a box of chocolates and offering her one. It was an embarrassing prospect but worth it to hear news of Vicky. "Tell your Mum I'd like to very much," Will said. The little girl was clearly disappointed at the sight of Will's foot in its big knitted sock. She had hoped for blood. She went off, chewing hard.

The Masons' Boxing Day tea was a vast spread, with three cakes, toast, muffins, rum butter, and plates of sandwiches. They welcomed him with the mixture of deference and shy curiosity to which Will was now becoming accustomed. He knew that he had to tell them about squadron life, about air fighting, and his last flight.

"Vicky was supposed to be home for Christmas," Mrs. Mason said surprisingly at the end of tea. "She was due for a week's leave, but her Channel boat was held up because of bad weather. But she'll be here tomorrow, and I know she'll want to see you, Will."

Will saw Vicky again on her knees in front of the fire, her long hair, darkened by the rain, spread out to dry. She had brushed it with brisk strokes, and her laughter mingled with her mother's. Why should she want to see him?

"You've both grown up since last year," Mrs. Mason continued. "Don't forget that. Vicky's less wild and impulsive now. Less unsettled. She often writes about you. She's still very fond of you, you know, but thinks she's lost you forever because of her selfishness."

Will found it all quite unbelievable. Even that brief chance sight of her from the train had become no more than another of the painful imaginary glimpses he had had of Vicky—at night on his bunk, late in the evening at the bar, even when flying sometimes—since he had left Amplethwaite in the middle of a school day. The reality had become too remote as well as too painful and too elusive for consideration.

On the way home, Will considered his self-doubts only briefly. Self-doubts were things of the past. It was the quick decision that kept you alive. And hadn't Vicky's mother said, "She'll want to see you, Will"? He diverted to the vicarage, moving with practiced speed on his crutches in the dark. It was a duty call he would have had to make anyway. Will remembered the vicar's wife as a beautiful woman, tall and self-possessed. Her bereavement had aged her ten years. Will sat down briefly in the drafty hall and said the right things and told her about the squadron padre. Then he let her into his confidence and told her his plan. Could he borrow the vicar's motor bicycle, just for one day?

"Of course you can, dear. If you can make it work and if you can ride it with that poor leg."

Will knew what a fuss there would be, even before Vicky arrived at Amplethwaite. He would not get her alone for hours. And her parents were certain to meet her at Windermere station. The only answer was to intercept her before she arrived. And though he believed her mother and knew that Vicky, too, had grown up a lot, he knew she would still enjoy the surprise and the touch of dramatic flourish of an unplanned meeting.

Will allowed plenty of time and set off for Preston three hours before the train from London was due, at the last minute and, on a whimsical impulse, strapping his old leather belt around his greatcoat. He left the crutches behind. They were an awkward encumbrance on the Indian motor bicycle, and he would just have to hop. The vicar had kept his motor bicycle in fine tune, and it had lost none of its power. It was a crisp, sunny morning, and Will let the machine have its head on the road to Lancaster. It was as good as flying.

A few miles south of Lancaster, the engine suddenly stopped dead. This was far worse than engine failure in a Camel. He was almost immobile, he had no tools, and he had the most important train in the world to meet. He drew into the side of the road and dismounted. All he had was his penknife. He suspected the fuel feed and began work on the carburetor. It took him half an hour to disassemble it, cutting his finger and bending both blades of his knife. Half an hour had been lost by the time he found the blockage and cleared it, and with shaking fingers he began putting it together again.

Will raced away with the throttle wide open. He caught fleeting glimpses of cattle shying back at his approach and scattering across the fields as he went roaring by. A horse bolted with an irate farmer. A group of open-mouthed children flashed past, and he went into a long skid on a corner and nearly fell off.

The journey was a miniature replica of his war—fast and dangerous. Speed, speed, speed up the fells on his two flashing feet, down from the skies in a 150-mile-per-hour dive after the enemy in his Camel. Speed and the will to win. Speed and growing up fast. Both of them, Vicky and Will, spurred on by the needs and dangers of war.

He scarcely slowed down for the outskirts of Preston. There were three minutes to go before the train was due. As he approached the station, he remembered its layout and made a sudden decision. Through the goods yard, he could avoid the steps down to the platform. He turned off the main road, down a steep cobbled incline, to the crowded yard. Men were shouting and waving at him, but he took no notice. There was a train standing at the platform, and it was beginning to move forward as Will changed down into first gear and shot up the slope. With his hand hard on the horn, he drove the Indian down the edge of the platform, scattering passengers and porters and maneuvering around luggage trolleys.

Curious faces stared out at him from the windows. They

were all strangers. Will was in despair. She was here somewhere. He must stop the train. He must leap onto it and find her. There was one more coach before the tender. One of the windows was still down, and inside, in the center of the seat between two fat men, was Vicky. "Get your bag and jump," he called. "Quick!"

There was a tight knot of people right in front of Will, and he had to brake to a halt. But between their heads he saw that Vicky had reacted with great speed. The door of her compartment swung open, and she leaped down onto the platform, half falling before she regained her balance. She was without her bag, but they could collect that at Windermere later.

Vicky ran around the crowd toward him. Her wide-brimmed red boater had fallen off, and she was holding it, and her chestnut hair streamed out behind. "Oh, Will, what a wonderful idea! I hated that train." She was laughing, and her brown eyes were alight with excitement. She would have driven the Indian if Will had suggested it.

"Climb on behind before I get arrested," Will said.

Vicky climbed onto the pillion, after a little difficulty with her long dress and coat, and put her arms around Will's waist. "Let's make it a lovely long journey," she said into his ear.

This time Will was greeted with cheers by the men in the goods yard, and Vicky waved back with her boater.

Out on the open road, they tried to talk, but it was difficult above the sound of the big twin engine. So he turned off up a lane and stopped by a barn. Vicky helped him through the gate, and he hopped toward a pile of winter hay.

Vicky stood looking down at him, her head on one side, unsmiling. "Poor foot," she said.

"You've seen a lot worse than this."

"Yes, of course, and at least you've got it. But it was such a wonderful fast foot."

"Not fast enough for you," said Will, watching her carefully. She was lovelier than ever. That mouth! Those brown eyes—solemn now as she gazed back.

"I was a very silly schoolgirl," she said earnestly. "And very cruel, and I've hated myself whenever I've thought about it ever since." She sat down beside him. "But I mustn't say I don't love winners anymore. Because that's not quite true." She was smiling again, and Will saw a new softness in the smile. "And it's not tactful either, considering what a lot of winning you've been doing."

Will was about to protest, but he had misjudged her, for she added quickly, "But I've learned not to chat away about gallantry and oh, you brave boys. I know how nearly everyone hates it. So we needn't say any more about how brave you are—"

"I don't think we need say any more about anything. Or perhaps about one thing." He seized her arm and pulled her down beside him. Their cold faces came together, and his lips roamed slowly through a tangle of hair all around her face, closing about her lips.

They remained like this for a long time, until the sound of a plane made Vicky lift her head. "Spying," she said.

"It's very lonely up there," said Will. "I don't blame him."

She pulled him up onto his good leg and wrapped his arm around her shoulder for support. "I bet you do this to all your patients," said Will.

"Only the deserving ones." The plane was still there, circling slowly at five hundred feet. "Let him have his fun," she said and reached for both his arms. They kissed until his leg began to give way and he had to hold on to the gate.

"I know someone who asked you to marry him the first

time you walked into his ward. Impetuous fellow, but he had good judgment. I might wait a bit longer but not much longer."

He did not discover that his belt was missing until he hung his greatcoat up in the hall cupboard late that evening.

GLOSSARY

aero engine power plant of an airplane

airframe structure of an airplane

Albatros German scout, or fighter airplane

Aldis sight telescopic gunsight

Archie slang for German antiaircraft fire

Aviatik Austrian-built scout, or fighter airplane

Avro British scout, or fighter airplane

balloons gas-filled balloons used for observing artillery fire and secured to the ground by cables

biplane airplane with two wings

Blériot French scout, or fighter airplane

Blighty slang for *England*

breeches legwear designed to hold the calf tightly for convenience in a cramped cockpit

Camel British scout, or fighter airplane

castor oil an additive to a plane's fuel

Clerget rotary French aero engine (power plant of an airplane)

C.O. Commanding Officer

Croix-de-Guerre French decoration for bravery

D.H.2 British scout, or fighter airplane

D.H.4 British scout, or fighter airplane

dihedral degree of angle of an airplane's wing

doped canvas surface covering of an airplane over the wooden frame, doped to draw it tight

D.S.O. Distinguished Service Order, a British decoration for bravery

elevator hinged section of an airplane's wing, which controls its bank, or tilt

Farman, Maurice man for whom Farman Shorthorn is named

Farman Shorthorn French-designed scout, or fighter airplane, which is also used for training pilots; *see also* Rumpty

Fee (F.E.2b) British scout, or fighter airplane

firing ring form of trigger for machine gun

fitter mechanic responsible for an airplane's engine

Fokker Dutch-designed German scout, or fighter airplane

Halberstadt German scout, or fighter airplane

Handley Page bomber large British bombing airplane

Harry Tates slang for F.E.8 British bombing airplane

holding opposite rudder (in a spin) pressing the foot-controlled rudder in the opposite direction to the spin of an airplane

Immelmann a half-loop maneuver used to gain height

jumping slang for surprising an intended victim

kite slang for *airplane*

Lewis gun machine gun

loop-the-loop a maneuver in which the airplane dives and completes a full circle

Martinsydes British scout, or fighter airplane

Mauser German gun

M.C. Military Cross, a British decoration for bravery

M.O. Medical Officer

Pfalz German scout, or fighter airplane

pip buttonlike insignia of rank

Pup British scout, or fighter airplane

pusher scout airplane with propeller behind engine, pushing rather than pulling

revs revolutions, or turns, of an engine's crankshaft

R.F.C. Royal Flying Corps

rigger mechanic responsible for an airplane but not the engine

rotary engine airplane engine with fixed crankshaft and rotating cylinders and propeller

roundel round, three-colored identification mark on sides and wings of British, French, and American airplanes

R.T.O. Railroad Travel Officer, who is responsible for travel arrangements

Rumpler German scout, or fighter airplane

Rumpty slang for *Farman Shorthorn*

S.E.5 British scout, or fighter airplane

Sopwith British company that designed and built airplanes including the Camel and Pup

Spandau German machine gun

spinner center piece of an airplane's propeller

splitarse maneuverable, responsive

square-bashing slang for *drill* and marching on the parade ground

torque reverse thrust on the direction of a plane caused by the spinning propeller

tractor biplane airplane with propeller in front of engine, the orthodox position

triplane airplane with three wings

u.s. unserviceable

V.C. Victoria Cross, a British decoration for bravery

Vickers gun British machine gun

wind sock large, hollow canvas tube that indicates to a pilot the direction and strength of the wind